To Kill the Valko Kid

Retired marshal Clem Everett rides into Sioux City a few moments after the infamous bounty hunter Johnny Sunset arrived and it was not long before Clem discovers that the man known as the Sunset Kid is only there to claim the reward money on his old pal Valko.

From an arrangement made way back, Clem knows Valko is due to appear in the city that night. The clock is ticking toward midnight and there is no way to warn his friend that the deadliest bounty hunter in the West is intent on gunning him down. Time is up for the Valko kid. . . .

To Kill the Valko Kid

Michael D. George

A Black Horse Western

ROBERT HALE · LONDON

◉ Michael D. George 2013
First published in Great Britain 2013

ISBN 978-0-7198-0881-4

Robert Hale Limited
Clerkenwell House
Clerkenwell Green
London EC1R 0HT

www.halebooks.com

Typeset by
Derek Doyle & Associates, Shaw Heath
Printed and bound in Great Britain by
CPI Antony Rowe, Chippenham and Eastbourne

Dedicated to Candice and Suzy with love and gratitude

ONE

Another day was dying. A victim to the inevitable coming of night. Soon it would be people who also breathed their last as they tasted the insanity of hot lead and a well-honed blade. The sky had turned to a deep crimson above the vast expanse of range which surrounded the lone horseman. Only fresh blood could have equalled its hellish hue as the sun finally sank below the distant mountain range and once again allowed the coming of nightfall. Ribbons of black rippling clouds spread across the scarlet heavens like sidewinders seeking refuge from the fire which filled the big sky.

Like a heart pumping its last drops of blood the red sky ultimately began to fade before the onslaught of a thousand eager stars.

The poetic might have seen majesty in the beautiful scene which engulfed the remote land dotted with countless homesteads but not the horseman who dragged back on his reins and balanced in his stirrups. He saw nothing but more innocent victims to use as his depraved, merciless soul desired. There were always men to kill and females to use in any way he so desired.

A guttural laugh filled the cooling air beneath his wide black hat brim. It was not the laugh of a happy man but rather the sound only the insane make when pondering upon their next outrage. His eyes narrowed as he slid the bandanna up over his face in order to lend credence to the lies he had lived by for so very long. Those who set eyes upon him and survived must not be able to see that he was far older than the innocent man he pretended to be.

Another chilling noise left his mouth. This time it was guarded by the black cloth before his face. He stared down at the land in front of him. So many things to do, he told himself. So many people to kill and to leave soiled.

There were the lights of a town across the range, almost opposite his high perch atop the dusty ridge. A town he would get to later. After he had satisfied his animal cravings in one of the small, almost deserted homesteads between it and him.

The land just south of Sioux City was fertile. Countless small homesteads were scattered across its black dirt, where honest souls scraped a living and prayed for help against the brutal elements.

Like an eagle on a high thermal the horseman studied everything before him in search of the weakest of the weak. It was hard to choose which of the small structures was the best target for him. So many small glimmers of light spilled out on to the eerie moonlit soil. Each little building offered something he craved like a drunkard craves hard liquor. Each held the prospect of females.

Again the cruel eyes drifted up from the small wooden structures and burned across the distance until they focused on the settlement. A thousand fireflies could not have equalled the strange glowing of the town's lantern light. With each heartbeat it was getting darker and colder but the rider did not seem to either notice or care. His mind was on other things.

Sioux City had profited over the years from the sweat and toil of the people who farmed the land which surrounded it. It had a railroad spur which once a week brought a train in to and out of the otherwise remote land. For most of its days the city had been quiet compared to other similar settlements.

That was about to change.

For the first time in its brief history Sioux City was about to understand the true meaning of the term Wild West. For soon trouble would be headed towards its quiet structures. Trouble in human forms.

One of these was the rider who falsely called himself the Valko Kid. A man who had been created by the Devil himself to do his bidding. Yet this man was nothing like the youngster he feigned to be.

There were no depths of evil this creature would not sink to in the comforting knowledge that the innocent Valko would end up being blamed for it.

The rider steadied his horse. Grunting laughter filtered through his raised bandanna.

The man who was clad in black and rode an almost white dapple-grey stallion knew that whatever he did, it would be blamed upon the far younger Valko. The real Valko: the man he had ruined and turned into a wanted outlaw.

The rider looped a leg over the cantle of his saddle and held his reins tightly as he stared down at the closest of the small buildings bathed in the bluish hue of the almost full moon.

As was his insane ritual he moved to his saddle-bags, pulled out a bag of chalk and started to cover the grey marks on his horse until it appeared to be totally white.

White like the stallion he wanted any witnesses to believe it to be. White like the horse belonging to the true Valko Kid, the innocent scapegoat for his misdeeds. Another cruel, mocking grunt came from the deadly man as he thought about the young Valko.

The kid whose life and reputation he had

destroyed for more than ten years.

He returned the chalk bag and patted his hands together until the white powder floated and disappeared into the moonlight.

The real Valko would never be able to prove his innocence as long as his evil shadow kept one step ahead of him. Whilst Valko hunted him the law hunted Valko.

His eyes narrowed. He stared hard at the nearest small house, made of mud and crude timber. It had a tin chimney protruding from its roof of cut sod.

There was smoke whispering from the blackened stack.

Someone was down there, he thought.

Someone with little or no protection from any visitors such as himself. A wider grin crossed his brutal face beneath the black bandanna.

He gathered his reins and stepped back into a stirrup. He hoisted himself up on to his saddle. He was ready. Ready to satisfy his lust or kill. It did not matter which.

Whoever it was down there inside that small house he was going to use them. Use them as he had used countless others cut from their honest, innocent cloth. If there were men inside there he would kill them and steal whatever possessions suited him. If there were females inside there, he would service them and if they objected he would end their lives swiftly.

11

He thrust his spurs back.

The now well-disguised grey stepped down the ridge towards the adobe. He could smell the fragrant aroma of cooking but it was not his belly that he wished to satisfy.

Dust floated upward behind the hoofs of the horse as its ruthless master guided it towards the dwelling. The closer he got the stronger the aroma of bacon frying became.

He was hungry for many things.

Food was only just one of them. There were far more pressing desires burning inside his unwholesome craw. Needs which most men would simply tolerate and subdue. But the deadly rider, whom the true Valko Kid had christened the Shadow, was not like decent men. The scent of the unknowing female filled his nostrils and fuelled him with a craving more potent than any drug found in the opium dens of most towns and cities.

When he had an itch he made damn sure it got scratched, whatever the consequences and price others might have to pay. Any objections were always met with the same brutal resolution. He sucked in the air through the black mask and knew that soon his corrupt soul would have another notch. Another innocent would soon be added to the countless others he had soiled over the years.

Silently the Shadow pulled back on his reins. The

well-disguised horse was brought to a stop close to
the east wall of the tiny shack. The burning eyes of its
master darted all around the moonlit scene from
above the bandanna and below the pulled-down hat
brim. He could see for miles in every direction across
the swaying grassland.

There was no one close.

If there was a man belonging to this small home-
stead he was within the confines of the tiny structure
before him. The Shadow flicked the loops of his
guns' hammers and swiftly checked that both his
guns were fully loaded, their hammers resting upon
a chamber with a fresh .45 bullet.

The only sound came from the hens inside their
small shed close to the rear wall of the shack. They
were well protected from foxes and coyotes, he
thought. Whoever was within the shack was probably
nowhere near as safe.

He eased himself up off the saddle and slowly
greeted the ground with his boots. He led the horse
around the ramshackle hut until he was glaring at its
only door. Lamplight spilled out from all the cracks
and gaps around its in frame.

The Shadow felt himself drawn like a moth to a
naked flame towards the splintered illumination.
Without a moment's hesitation he silently tied his
reins to the only upright, rested his wrists on the
grips of his holstered weapons and began his

approach. He could hear the alluring voice from within. A female voice humming a long-forgotten melody as she went about making the evening meal. There was no talking. Just the sound of a happy woman as she saw to her nightly chores.

The bandanna concealed the sickening grin of the voyeur.

He turned once more and cast his eyes on the land around him in search of the man he felt was out there somewhere. Her man. A man the Shadow would undoubtedly kill if he existed or showed himself.

But there was still no sign of anyone who might prevent him from doing what he intended doing. The only living creature he could see was a milk cow tethered to fence poles close to the henhouse.

His eyes screwed up against the moonlight. The ground around the small building was filled with plants, a fertile garden filled with vegetables. The garden probably gave these people all they required to keep them alive in this unforgiving land.

The Shadow swung on his heels and stared at the door.

The door was the only thing between him and the woman, whom he could smell as well as the frying bacon. Tantalizing flashes of movement interrupted the lamp light as she moved back and forth around the tiny interior of the shack. He heard the sound of tin plates being placed on a wooden surface.

The meal was almost ready.

He edged forward until the door touched his hat brim. He then paused and inhaled quietly as many atrocities raced through his twisted mind. Soon there would be another sin to add to all the others.

He was now looking into the one-room shack: watching her move around in total ignorance of his presence. He studied her carefully. A woman of maybe twenty or thirty years? It was hard to tell with women who lived on the ranges. The elements were cruel to females. The Shadow liked what he saw. She had a good figure. It had shape. Curves where women were meant to have them.

Then his eyes looked at her body again.

His mask concealed the smile.

She was alone.

The second plate meant nothing.

The Shadow stroked the grips of his guns and teased their exposed hammers. He knew that when it came to a showdown he had never once met anyone who was faster on the draw than himself.

Was there such an animal? A man capable of out-drawing one of the most lethal creatures west of the Pecos.

A bead of sweat rolled down the side of his face from the band of his hat. The black bandanna soaked it up as he leaned against the brittle wood of the door.

He pushed the door and it obeyed.

It creaked as it swung inward on its hinges and he walked past it into the shack.

For a moment the woman did not even raise her head. She continued to stir the contents of the skillet whilst humming a tune of her own creation.

'About time ya got here,' she said.

The Shadow did not speak. He just watched her.

Then her beautiful eyes flashed away from the small stove and locked on to the uninvited intruder who stood just inside the dirt floor boundary that separated the inside from the outside.

Her expression changed. Suddenly it began to reflect the horror which was welling up within her. She slowly turned to face him. Her hands still held on to the skillet as she tried to bluff the masked figure into thinking she was unafraid.

'Who are you?' she heard herself asking. 'What are you doing here in my home?'

He did not answer at first. He stepped closer.

'Who in tarnation are ya?' Her voice rose high and loud as she started to shake. 'A stinking outlaw by the looks of that mask ya hiding behind.'

'They call me Valko,' the Shadow lied. 'The Valko Kid.'

'What you want with me?'

His eager hands tore at the calico dress. Countless

16

washes had made the fabric weak. It disintegrated.

The Shadow moved closer. 'I want you.'

TWO

Ten miles south of the range and the sprawling Sioux City another horseman was making his way through the darkness. This rider was utterly different from the man who had made a career out of masquerading as the Valko Kid. The real Valko eased back on his reins and allowed his white stallion to rest as he surveyed the fertile landscape which surrounded him. Valko dismounted and dropped his long leathers to the ground. He was tired but knew he could not rest if he were to keep the appointment he had made with his old friend Clem Everett. He stretched, then checked the legs of his magnificent stallion before removing his black Stetson and placing it before the thirsty horse.

Valko removed one of his canteens from the saddle horn and filled the bowl of his hat with the precious liquid. He watched the tired horse drink, then took a mouthful of water himself.

'Sure wish this was a cold beer, Snow,' Valko said before screwing the stopper back on the canteen and replacing it on the high saddle horn. He rubbed the dust from his face and than looked around them.

It had been a hard ride and one he had not wanted to make but Valko was always true to his word. He had arranged to meet his old pal on the first of April in Sioux City and that was what he intended doing. He thought about all of the years he had lost trying to outrun one posse after another.

Wanted dead or alive and worth $25,000 had made him one of the most prized outlaws in the West.

'One day I'll catch that varmint who ruined my life, Snow,' Valko said as he lifted the hat back off the ground and placed it on his head. The cold droplets of water which traced down his face and neck felt good. 'Then you and me will be able to rest up and not have folks shooting at us.'

The Kid gave a sigh.

He had said the same words for over ten years.

Valko no longer believed them.

He looked up at the stars and tried to work out in which direction he had to steer his faithful mount. He grabbed the saddle horn and poked his left boot into the stirrup. He mounted the tall animal, then paused for a moment. He was not sure where he was but reckoned a town as big as Sioux City was said to be could not be easily missed.

'Reckon we'd best head north,' he muttered.

Then he heard something.

It sounded like a stampede. The air was rumbling with the noise of hoofs. A lot of hoofs thundering across the ground somewhere close.

'What in tarnation is that, Snow?' Valko asked the horse who had also heard the noise.

He stood in his stirrups and looked all around him. The Kid kept turning his mount as his eyes vainly searched the horizon in all directions.

Then he saw them.

At least twenty riders.

'Damn!' Valko cursed as he focused on the lead horseman, a rider on a large pinto. 'That's the posse that was dogging our tails two days ago, Snow.'

Valko swung the horse around in a circle as he tried to work out which was the best way to go. Before he had made up his mind the shots rang out. He pulled his reins up to his chest and squinted through the half-light at the riders. Gunsmoke now hung over the bunch.

More shots rang out.

So far their bullets were falling short, Valko thought. So far they were just out of range with their six-shooters. That would change if any of the approaching posse started to use their rifles. The Kid dragged his reins to his left and gave out a chilling call that his mount understood.

'Go, boy. Ride, Snow. Ride fast.'

The muscular white stallion had never once in all its days let its young master down. It thundered in the opposite direction to where the score of horse-men were coming from.

Each long stride of the huge horse seemed to stretch the gap between the hunters and the hunted.

Valko looked over his shoulders. The dust kicked up from Snow's shoes was acting like a shield. He could no longer see the posse but he could see the flashes of their guns as one after another tried his luck.

Bullets were hissing in the night air.

So far none had been able to catch up with the Valko Kid. Then a volley of shots cut through the air above him. The Kid started to swing his reins and whip the ground close to his mount's tail.

'Keep going, boy,' Valko implored the horse. 'They got their carbines out and they got our range.'

The magnificent white stallion charged powerfully across the range with the twenty riders behind them. Valko turned the horse and encouraged it on. The horse leapt twenty feet down into a dusty draw. The narrow tree-lined draw was shrouded in darkness.

The rising moon had yet to find it with its eerie light.

The young rider stood high in his stirrups and

leaned over the neck of the galloping white mount beneath him. Then he heard the posse scrambling down into the draw behind his horse. Valko looked back.

He saw them through the dry dust that hung in his wake.

The riders could only ride two abreast in the narrow confines of the draw as they chased their valuable prey. The Kid knew that meant only the two lead horsemen could risk firing their weaponry at him.

The thought had no sooner traced a trail through his mind than two rifle shots rang out. Both bullets cut red tapers through the darkness which surrounded him. The Kid continued to urge his trusty mount on as the draw twisted and turned. Then he heard two more rifle shots. One hit a wall of sod ahead of his charging horse. The other was so close it cut through the sleeve of his black shirt and grazed his left bicep.

It felt as though his arm had suddenly been set alight.

Valko gritted his teeth and fought the pain as he steered the horse up an embankment and back on to higher ground.

He sat down and began to work the reins in his hands to make sure the white stallion did not slow its pace.

'Keep going, Snow,' the Kid yelled into the

pricked ears of the big horse.

The moonlight was now his worst enemy.

Its light illumined everything around him.

Valko swung the tails of his long leathers again. It sounded like a hive of enraged hornets to the faithful horse. It meant they had to keep charging ahead no matter what the cost. Then Valko saw a small gathering of trees a hundred yards to his right. He leaned back against his cantle, and turned the mighty stallion and cracked the long reins against the ground.

Suddenly he heard the sound of the posse as they struggled up the embankment. Valko did not look back. He dared do nothing but concentrate on the rugged land that faced him.

Then shots again shook the night air.

Valko rode through the trees and pulled back on his reins. As dust spilled over horse and master the young rider peered through the trees at the posse.

'There got to be at least twenty of the critters, Snow,' he said. Then he twisted and turned on his saddle until he saw a steep rise a quarter of a mile from the tiny groove.

The hill Valko was studying rose about fifty feet higher than the ridge upon which he and his mount were resting and between them there was a gap of about twenty feet. A gap which would have to be jumped to reach the rest of the trail.

The Kid knew it would take a mighty confident

horseman to attempt to jump that gap. A man who trusted the horse beneath his saddle with his very life.

To make a mistake would be catastrophic.

Then bullets started to ping off the group of trees which guarded both horse and rider.

'C'mon, Snow. Let's see how brave them *hombres* really are.' Valko urged the horse into action. The powerful creature bolted away from their brief sanctuary and headed straight towards the rise which led to the broken trail.

The stallion's hoofs were eating up the dry ground beneath them. Faster and faster it went as its master steered it towards the high rise, to the place where the trail had a really big gap in it.

Bullets were flying all around the expert rider but Valko knew that even their best marksman could not hit them now. Once again the white stallion had proved its worth and managed to thunder away from its master's enemies' bullets.

The Kid could see the point of no return getting closer with each stride of his mount. He rose up off the saddle and gripped the reins tightly as they approached the spot where the trail abruptly ended.

'C'mon, Snow,' the Kid screamed out.

The land levelled out for the last stretch towards the broken trail. The place where the very middle of a natural bridge had fallen down into the gulch

24

below them.

Then to his horror Valko realized that the gap was far wider that it had appeared from down on the range. It had to be close to twenty-five feet of nothing but fresh air directly ahead of his mount. Maybe even thirty feet, Valko judged, as Snow kept ploughing on regardless.

Could the stallion make that jump?

Such a feat had never been asked of the powerful stallion before, the Kid thought.

Valko hung on as the horse lifted off into the night air. The terrified rider glanced down. He could see the swirling starlit water down below them in the ravine.

The stallion had used its muscular back legs to leap like a coiled spring up into the air. The Kid felt his body float up from the saddle. Only his grip on the reins and his boots jammed in the stirrups were preventing him from falling to his death.

The moonlight illuminated the ground on the opposite side of the hill. It was getting closer as the intrepid horse began to fall from the air towards it.

The Kid closed his eyes, then he felt the violent impact as the horse's hoofs found solid ground once more. The rider bounced like a child's ball before settling on the hand-tooled saddle. It took every scrap of the youngster's resolve to remain atop his still thundering horse as the animal raced down the slope away from the perilous cliff edge that it had just negotiated.

To Valko's surprise the white stallion had not even lost a stride. It kept on galloping. When the horse reached the cover of an outcrop of jagged boulders Valko drew rein and brought his mount to a grinding halt.

Dust swept up into the moonlight.

The snorting horse lowered its head as its master turned and looked back. The Kid could see every man of the posse lined up at the very top of the deadly chasm far behind them. Not one of their followers had even dared to try and jump the ravine. They were all marooned on the other side of the broken trail, knowing they would have to take a long detour before they could continue their chase. The score of frustrated horsemen continued to fire their rifles vainly at the wanted man who was so close and yet so far away.

Every bullet fell short of its target.

Valko patted the neck of the horse.

'Reckon they'll not give us any more grief, Snow.'

They rode on for Sioux City.

THREE

Sioux City had only one main avenue, but countless side streets meandered away from its centre like the twisted hind legs of a pack of hound dogs.

Lantern light spilled from every store front and splashed out on to the faces of those who milled together in search of the town's more dubious nocturnal entertainment. It was another night identical to all those which had gone before it. Another night which drew a certain type of people out from their respective hiding-places. These were the people who rested during the hours of daylight and only truly came to life when the smell of coal-tar lanterns filled the night air.

Saloons, gambling houses and the numerous brothels came alive when match flames were touched to lantern and lamp wicks.

Yet no one realized the horror which was happening out on the range or the danger which might be headed their way should the Shadow aim his horse towards Sioux City.

Then the approaching locomotive made its presence known as its driver let rip on its whistle. The train was winding its way through the ramshackle streets towards the stockyard and the countless beef steers which had been penned there in anticipation of its arrival. Fragments of red cinders flew heavenward from its stack. They floated towards the stars set upon the black canvas stretched above the vast range.

Most of the town ignored the regular visitor, as though it was invisible. The locomotive kept on moving regardless towards the stock pens. Only those who worked in and around the railhead paid any heed to the whistle's signal.

Steam squirted from both sides of the many-wheeled engine as it laboured towards the depot. Smoke billowed from its high stack in frustrated clouds of raw power.

The long train came to an abrupt halt. Men appeared like phantoms from every shadow to greet it. Men who were employed to fill with expertise its cavernous cars with the white-faced cattle. With torches held high the men proceeded to execute their duties. The large wooden sides of the cars were released from their restraints and fell on sturdy hinges to the ground, creating ramps. These allowed the steers to be encouraged up into the wagons which would take them to their fate.

The last two cars were different from those which had been designed to hold steers. One was a passenger car, the other was built to hold mail and a hefty safe. A well-armed guard kept the safe company. A solitary conductor saw to the needs of the passengers.

Yet this night the train had only one fare payer: a man whose innocent looking appearance belied the fact that he was the most ruthless bounty hunter ever to set foot in Sioux City. As he stepped down from the passenger car his eyes never stopped surveying the unfamiliar location. Apart from the torches spread around the pens the rest of the depot was shrouded in total darkness. He knew all too well that a million shadows could conceal a million foes.

If anyone had studied the stranger they would have realized it was not deceptive youthful looks that told the story of a man's worth. It was the kind of shooting rig he sported; this man had the most lethal of shooting rigs imaginable.

A run-of-the-mill holstered .45 hung on his favoured left side whilst a uniquely adapted double-barrelled shotgun was sheathed in a specially designed holster on his right. The weapon had been modified by a blacksmith years before to be as useful as a handgun.

The bounty hunter drew a cigar from his pocket and placed it between his teeth. He did not light it.

Johnny Sunset had been called many things in his time but friendly had never been one of them. To most he was worse than those he hunted. Even lawmen feared the innocent face of the man who had become known as the Sunset Kid because he had brought many sunsets to an awful lot of outlaws just to collect the bounty on their wanted heads.

Sunset rested his saddle-bag on the ground next to his high-necked boots. He pulled his gloves tight over his hands until the leather felt like a second skin. He then retrieved the bags and flung them over his right shoulder, so that one satchel rested on his back whilst the other lay across his chest. He started to walk to where the glimmer of glowing coal-tar lanterns beckoned.

He crossed the shining rail tracks and headed through the winding streets and alleyways. Many eyes secretly studied the stranger on his way to the heart of Sioux City. Not one person approached him, though.

Youthful and innocent as he appeared, Johnny Sunset was obviously dangerous. Far more dangerous than most who visited the remote settlement.

Every confident stride of his long legs took Sunset

deeper into Sioux City. Took him closer to where the tinny sound of pianos and the smell of stale tobacco hung in the air.

The bounty hunter adjusted his saddle-bags to distribute the weight of each of its satchels more evenly, then he entered a dark unlit alley. The sound grew louder and the smell grew stronger when suddenly his progress was blocked by a huge man almost as wide as the alley itself.

The man slowly turned to face the bounty hunter. As he turned Johnny Sunset caught the briefest glimpse of something in the lowered right hand.

There was no mistaking a cocked six-shooter with a seven-inch-long barrel.

'I thought it was you, Sunset,' the deep voice uttered as faint traces of starlight lit up the unblinking eyes. 'Even before the train stopped I done seen ya waiting to get off. Long time since we locked horns.'

'Yep, a mighty long time.' Sunset kept staring at the hand as it crept up the wide body of the man.

'So ya recalls me?'

'Nope,' the bounty hunter replied honestly. 'Who are ya?'

There was a pause. A long snorting pause. Then the man rested his hand against his wide chest. The long-barrelled gun was ready for action. Ready to kill.

'Ya mean ya don't recall me, Sunset?' The low voice sounded offended. 'After all we done meant to one another I'd have thought ya would recall me.'

'Bearclaw Jacobs,' Sunset heard himself say.

Jacobs smiled.

'Yep. I knew ya couldn't forget me, Kid.' The figure continued to fill the narrow lane. The gun kept moving on the huge chest.

'How could I forget ya? Not after I killed ya brother for two thousand dollars on his head,' Sunset said as he flexed the fingers of his left hand over the grip of his holstered Colt. 'I never hurt you though, Bearclaw.'

'Only coz I didn't have me no bounty on my head,' Jabobs snapped back. 'If I'd been worth just five bucks you'd have killed me. Right?'

'Dead right, Bearclaw.'

'But I got me a price on my head now.' Jacobs took a step towards the bounty hunter. 'I'm worth an even thousand bucks since I killed me a deputy over in Waco, just coz the star-packing bastard reminded me of you.'

Faster than the blink of an eye both well-armed men went for the kill. Jabobs swung his gun around and squeezed its trigger just as the Sunset Kid drew and fired. Two deafening flashes lit up the alley for the briefest moment.

Both men staggered backwards for a few steps.

Bearclaw Jacobs had gone to drag back on his gun hammer again when the gun slipped from his grip and fell to the ground. Only then did he realize that the bounty hunter's bullet had hit him dead centre. He glanced down and saw the blood pumping from the smoking hole in his shirt.

'Ya killed me,' Jacobs growled. 'But my shot was true. I never done miss anything I aim at. Never. My bullet hit you in the heart.

Sunset nodded, then holstered his Colt. He walked towards the man mountain and pointed to the leather satchel hanging over his own chest. A bullet hole smoked in the swollen bag. It marked the place where Jacob's shot had hit it.

'Ya aim was perfect as always, Bearclaw,' Sunset said. 'If'n I wasn't carrying my bag I figure your bullet would have gone right through my heart. Just like mine did to yours.'

Jacobs dropped on to his knees. Now blood was filling his mouth as his questioning eyes burned into the bounty hunter.

'What ya got in that satchel, Kid?'

'Just an old skillet, Bearclaw,' Sunset replied. He watched as the dead outlaw buckled and fell on to his face at his feet. The bounty hunter laughed and stepped over the large carcass. 'A thousand bucks, huh? Thank ya kindly, Bearclaw. Give my regards to your brother.'

33

Sunset chewed on the cigar in the corner of his mouth and then struck a match to light it without missing a stride as he continued on towards the main street. A line of smoke trailed over his shoulder as he kept on heading towards the ever-growing sound of people having fun.

When he reached the main street he paused. Sunset filled his lungs with smoke and grinned at the sight of the sign directly opposite the alley.

'Sheriff's Office,' Sunset said through a line of smoke.

FOUR

Johnny Sunset focused on the small well-kept building set amid so many larger ones. Its lanterns were dim compared to all the others spread out along the street. As was usual, the lawman who occupied the office had no reason to draw unwanted attention to its existence. Sunset waited for a break in the constant traffic of vehicles, horsemen and people on foot and then started across the lantern-lit sand.

'Well, whoever wears the star sure likes to keep his head down,' Sunset muttered with a wry grin. 'Just what I was looking for. A real tame lawman with no backbone.'

Riders and buckboards, men and women on foot moved in every conceivable direction between the bounty hunter and his goal, yet Sunset did not seem to notice any of them. He walked straight to where he could see the light escaping from the single window's weathered blinds.

He stepped up on to the boardwalk outside the office's painted door and tossed his cigar aside.

He gripped and turned the handle.

He entered and paused as a seated man looked up from behind a desk at him. The man's eyes studied the bounty hunter, but lingered on the strange weapon on Sunset's right hip.

'Who are you?' the sheriff asked.

'Johnny Sunset.'

There was a long pause as the sheriff sucked in air. 'The Sunset Kid?'

The bounty hunter nodded. 'Yep. That's what some folks call me, old-timer.'

'I heard of ya,' the sheriff said. 'I don't want no killing in Sioux City, Kid. Ya hear me?'

'Too late.' Sunset shrugged. 'I reckon ya already owes me a bounty of a thousand bucks.'

The sheriff rose to his feet. 'What?'

'I killed a critter named Bearclaw Jacobs in the alley yonder.' The Kid sighed, sat down on a hard-backed chair. 'He nearly done for me and would have if I hadn't been sporting this as a vest.' He patted one of the saddle-bags.

The lawman returned his rump back to his own chair. 'Why'd ya do that?'

'He started it.' Sunset grinned as he poked a finger in the bullet hole in his bag. 'Unfortunately for old Bearclaw, I finished it.'

The sheriff rubbed a sleeve along his brow. 'I don't like having killing in my town. You understand me?'

'Yep, I surely do.' Sunset looked at the man seated across the desk from him. 'Thing is, I'm a bounty hunter and I kill for a living.'

'Not in my town.'

'I repeat myself.' Sunset stood up. 'Too late. Any varmint that draws on me is fresh meat as far as I'm concerned. I kill anyone with a price tag on his head and I also kill anyone who tries to kill me. Whoever they are.'

'Get out of my town.' The lawman waved his hand.

Sunset stared at the wall covered with Wanted posters beside the door and poked his gloved finger on one of them. 'Not until I kill me this critter, Sheriff.'

The lawman rose as the bounty hunter stepped out on to the boardwalk. He moved to the posters and stared at the one the younger man had jabbed.

'You're after the Valko Kid?'

'Yep.' Sunset lit another cigar and nodded through a cloud of smoke. 'Don't go fretting none. I'll be back in the morning for my thousand dollars.'

Sheriff Chuck Bristow marched out into the cool evening air and was about to start shouting when he heard a familiar voice over his shoulder. He swung on his heels and stared at the horseman who had just reined in at the hitching rail.

'I said ya ought to be wearing a hat, Chuck,' the rider remarked as he looped his leg over the cantle of his saddle and slowly lowered his long frame to the ground.

'Clem Everett.' Bristow gasped in surprise. 'I heard ya was dead. Dead and buried.'

'Not hardly.' The retired marshal secured his reins to the hitching pole and encouraged his tall gelding to drink from the trough. 'What's gotten my old deputy so all-fired up? You look ready to burst.'

Bristow pointed down the street but the throng of people blocked the view of the bounty hunter as he meandered through them. 'There. Did ya see him, Clem?'

'See who?' Everett pulled his tobacco pouch from his vest pocket and slid a paper from it. 'I see me a whole bunch of folks. Whose gotten under ya collar?'

'The Sunset Kid.' The sheriff snorted as he poked at the air with his finger. 'Didn't ya see the bastard? He ain't bin in town more than five minutes and he's already killed somebody.'

Clem turned his friend to face him. 'Sunset? The bounty hunter?'

'Yeah. The stinking bounty hunter.' Bristow nodded firmly and his face grew crimson. 'I don't want no damn bounty hunter in my town. Them critters kill anything with a price on its head, no matter how small it is. As long as the poster has "Dead or Alive" printed on it, they start killing.'

'Why would Sunset be here in Sioux City?' Everett rubbed his whiskered jawline with his thumb. 'Seems a tad out of the way for most men in his profession.'

'He's after the Valko Kid.'

The expression on the face of the taller man changed. He was also here to find his friend Valko. 'You sure about that, Chuck boy?'

'Yep,' Bristow replied. 'He done bragged about it. He's here to kill the Valko Kid. With the cannon he's packing on his right hip I'd say he can do it. I never seen such a weapon before. It looked something like a scattergun, but it was holstered.'

Clem Everett walked into the well-lit office and rested a hip on the desk as he continued to roll his cigarette. Bristow followed and sat down. He recognized the expression on the retired marshal's face well.

'Why are you here, Clem?'

There was no reply.

FIVE

Clem Everett had never been a man to hide his feelings. He was of the breed of retired lawmen who always try to be straight-talking and straight-shooting. The trouble was, Everett had become the friend of a wanted outlaw a few years earlier, when the Valko Kid had saved his life with no regard to his own safety. The Kid had proved to Clem that he was innocent many times but neither man had been able to gather the evidence to remove the stain which had blighted the young man's life.

The law still said that Valko was an outlaw and no matter how hard the youngster had tried he had never managed to prove his innocence and clear his name. Wanted dead or alive with a $25,000 bounty on his head, Valko had become the prized target for many bounty hunters over the years, and so forced to hide. Clem knew that Valko's claim was genuine. The atrocities had been committed by a man who masqueraded as Valko.

Everett had actually seen the man: he had even fought the evil creature whom Valko had dubbed his 'Shadow'.

Yet how could Clem explain to his old deputy why he was so troubled by the fact that Johnny Sunset was hell-bent on claiming the reward money? How could the retired marshal tell Bristow that he had been riding with a man wanted dead or alive? That he was trying to find and capture the real deadly killer before Valko's luck finally ran out and a bullet ended his young friend's life.

There was another burning branding-iron tormenting the mind of the older man as he held his cup of coffee and inhaled its aroma. He had arranged months earlier to meet up with Valko in Sioux City on the first of April; now he needed to warn his young pal to stay away. It was impossible. There was no way he could get in touch with the elusive young Valko. No way to warn his friend that the legendary Johnny Sunset was waiting for him.

Now the black hands on the face of the wall clock moved ever closer to midnight. Midnight would not only bring another day but another month: April.

Clem sat on the hardbacked chair in the middle of the sheriff's office and stared through the steam of his coffee out into the still busy street as his old friend strapped on his gunbelt and checked his Peacemaker.

'Ya gonna stay here, Clem?' Bristow asked. He pulled his hat off the piles of unread posters which littered his desk and made his way to the open door. 'Stay here or stretch them long legs and join me on my rounds?'

A thousand thoughts had deafened Clem Everett. He had been pondering the words which the sheriff had uttered only an hour earlier. The words had chilled him to the marrow of his ancient bones. The most deadly bounty hunter in the West was in Sioux City in order to kill the Valko Kid.

For most retired lawmen the simple sentence would have been like water off a duck's back. It would not have meant a thing to them and secretly they might have been relieved that someone apart from themselves was going up against the infamous outlaw. But Everett was the one peace officer with whom the words stuck and lingered.

He knew of the injustice with which Valko had been maligned, and for the best part of two years he had ridden with him, vainly trying to find the real perpetrator of the abominable atrocities which had all been attributed to his young friend.

Clem looked at Bristow.

Could he tell him the truth? Should he? A lot of water had passed under the bridge since Bristow had been Everett's deputy. He could have told the young Chuck Bristow, but doubted that this grey-haired man would either understand or believe him.

The sound of the wall clock ticking seemed to grow louder in the small office. Clem lifted his coffee cup to his lips and swallowed the last dregs.

He had nearly died months earlier when he had been shot up by a posse who had mistaken him for the Valko Kid as he had ridden the outlaw's mighty white stallion. He had rested up in the town of War Smoke and had arranged to meet up with Valko in Sioux City at the beginning of April.

The retired lawman looked at the grubby calendar hanging on the back wall. This was the final day of March.

Clem knew that Valko would arrive any time after midnight.

Valko was never late.

The snapping of fingers drew the attention of the older man to the sheriff.

'I asked ya if'n ya staying here, Clem.' Bristow repeated his question. 'I know them old bones of yours must be hankering to find a soft mattress.'

Everett rose to his full height and strode across the office to the stove. He placed the tin cup down next to the blackened coffee pot and adjusted his wide-brimmed hat.

'Nope. I ain't tired, ya young galoot,' Clem

answered. 'I reckon I'll hold ya hand and walk around this town with you. We can have us a talk.'

'About what?' Bristow led his pal out into the street after closing and locking the office door.

'Hell.' Clem smiled as his mind kept brooding on the fact that Johnny Sunset was in town to kill his best friend. 'We got us about fifteen years to talk about. Ya must have done something in all them years worth bragging about?'

'Not hardly.' Bristow slid the key into his vest pocket. 'Ya still the old gossip, I see. Ya never could go half a buckboard ride without wanting to chat. That's bin ya problem, Clem. Ya talk and think too darn much. No good comes of either in my book.'

Clem glanced at his lathered-up horse. 'Where's the nearest livery stable, Chuck? Reckon I'd best get my old horse watered and grained after our little stroll.'

'Is that the same hoss ya used to ride when I was ya deputy, Clem?' the sheriff asked.

'Yep.' Clem nodded and came to walk beside the shorter man as they meandered along the board-walk. The sounds of riotous laughter ebbed and flowed like waves along the thoroughfare. It was far busier than most towns Everett had frequented.

'Ya sure got an awful lot of folks in Sioux City looking for a good time, Chuck,' Clem observed. 'Must be a gold mine or two around here someplace.'

44

'Cattle and sweet grass, Clem.' Bristow tapped the side of his nose. 'Fat steers are worth more than gold is back East, ya know.'

The two men continued on. They passed one saloon after another, each with its own aroma of stale sawdust, tobacco smoke and liquor. Females were plentiful, spilling out on to the boardwalks from the drinking holes and other well-patronized businesses. Everett touched his hat brim in acknowledgement to each and every one of them who fluttered her eye-lashes in his direction.

'Ya sure got a lot of ladies of the night around here, Chuck,' his companion said from the corner of his mouth as he kept nodding to all the painted faces.

'Least ya eyes are still working, old-timer.' Bristow laughed out loud.

They passed another saloon. Everett looked over the swing doors into the busy interior at the men and ladies going about their riotous endeavours.

'Ain't ya going inside any of these drinking holes, Chuck?'

'Nope,' Bristow replied. 'I only goes in them for two reasons. One is when I hear gun play. The other reason is to get my cut of the take.'

'Ya still on a percentage, huh?' Clem frowned dis-approvingly.

'Sure enough,' the sheriff admitted. 'Hell. I sure

don't wanna end up like all the other lawmen I've known over the years who managed to survive but ended up broke. When I quit this damn job I'm gonna retire in style, Clem.'

'Meaning me. Ya don't wanna end up like me.' Everett gave out a short sigh. 'Damned if I can argue with ya reasoning, boy.'

Bristow laughed out loud. 'Boy? That's the first time anyone called me that since we last rode together.'

The two stalwart figures were about to cross the busy street when they heard a commotion somewhere beyond the crowd and the traffic that was clogging up the long thoroughfare. Raised voices suddenly and without warning gave place to gunfire. A lot of gunfire.

'What in tarnation?' Bristow gasped.

'That's shooting, boy,' Clem snapped. 'Reckon ya ain't heard a whole heap of that in a while.'

A deafening volley eched off the façades of the wooden buildings along Main Street. Within a blink of an eye the people and vehicles filling the street had turned and were racing away from the sound of the shooting. Horses and wagons were whipped into action and thundered past the sheriff and the retired marshal. They were scattering as speedily as those on foot. Everyone was taking cover as more shots echoed along the street.

While hysterical people stampeded along the boardwalk in blind terror Clem held on to the upright of a porch, stepped on to a trough and hoisted himself up until he could see down the long street over the heads of the fleeing crowd.

'What ya see, Clem?' Bristow called.

'I see me a whole heap of gunsmoke, Chuck.' Clem jumped down and grabbed the sheriff's sleeve. 'C'mon.'

It was as if the two one-time colleagues had suddenly gone back twenty years in time. Countless times before today they had raced shoulder to shoulder towards the place from here everyone else seemed to be fleeing.

Clem Everett took the lead as he had always done, confident in the knowledge that he could trust his companion to cover his back.

The veteran lawmen pushed their way through the last group of hysterical people who came between themselves and their objective. The acrid aroma of gunsmoke lingered heavily and drew the two men to the place they sought.

In the middle of the street Johnny Sunset was standing over a wounded man, holding his Colt .45 in his left hand as smoke trailed from its barrel. The strange scattergun remained holstered and unused.

Sunset glanced at both men as they came to a halt and stood over the bleeding man. There was a smile

47

on the bounty hunter's face, which told both Bristow and Everett that this man had not finished. He was like a cat waiting for his mouse to dare to move before striking once more.

'Gents,' Johnny Sunset said without a hint of emotion in his deep voice.

The man on the ground looked up at Bristow. For the first time in his miserable life he was grateful for the sight of a tin star. He thought that the sheriff would be able to stop the bounty hunter from ending his misery.

'Ya gotta help me, Sheriff,' the wounded man pleaded.

'Quit belly-aching, Hec,' Sunset snarled. He carefully pulled three spent casings from his gun and replaced them with fresh bullets from his fancy belt. 'Ya knows ya wanted dead or alive. Ya also know that I don't cotton to bringing stinking outlaws like you in alive.'

Hec Colby tried to rise but the two well-placed bullets in his legs prevented anything so ambitious.

'Don't let him kill me, Sheriff. Please. Ya gotta stop this maniac from killing me. I quit. I'm finished.' the outlaw was nearly crying as his fingers clawed at the hard-packed ground.

'What the hell are ya doing, Sunset?' Bristow yelled at the bounty hunter as he and Clem stood above the blood-soaked man on the ground. 'Ya can't go shooting innocent folks like this.'

'Hec ain't no innocent, Sheriff,' Sunset replied. He snapped the gun shut and cocked its hammer once more before training it on the bloody man at Bristow's feet. 'He's wanted dead or alive in three territories, including this'un. Killed a preacher in the last town he visited. Ain't that right, Hec?'

The sheriff glanced down at Hec Colby. 'Is that right, Hec?'

Clem looked at the man who used to be his deputy. 'Don't ya ever look at the Wanted posters in ya office, Chuck?'

'I bin a tad busy,' the sheriff protested. 'Besides, there ain't never no trouble in Sioux City.'

Everett inhaled deeply. He stared at Johnny Sunset long and hard, as though trying to work out the weaknesses in the infamous bounty hunter. Yet no matter how hard he looked he saw no fragilities. Sunset was a killing machine just as his reputation had painted him.

'Ya like killing, Sunset?' Clem asked.

'Only when there's a pay-day attached to the critter I'm aiming my hogleg at, old-timer,' the bounty hunter retorted, spinning his handgun on his index finger. 'What's it to do with you anyway? Who are ya?'

'I ain't nobody,' Clem responded sharply. 'I'm just an old man who used to kill. Just like you.'

Johnny Sunset looked towards the sheriff. 'Another thing. Have ya had Bearclaw's body picked up yet, Sheriff? Best do it before dawn unless ya likes eating flies.'

Bristow looked flustered. 'I've had it carted off to the funeral parlour, boy. Hell, will ya stop killing folks for a while, Sunset? Give me a chance at catching up with ya slaughtering?'

'Ain't my fault ya damn slow.' Sunset kept looking at the outlaw on the ground.' He had hit him three times with three shots. Blood was pumping in all directions from the bullet holes.

'I needs me a doctor, Sheriff,' Colby screamed as he forced himself into a sitting position. 'I'm gonna die here while you old critters is talking.'

Bristow gritted his teeth and waved a hand at the bounty hunter. 'Just a minute there, Hec. Listen up, Sunset. . . .'

Ignoring the sheriff Sunset spat at Colby. 'Ya ain't gonna live long enough to get to a doc, Hec.'

Suddenly, without warning, Hec Colby reached under his bloody vest and produced a gore-covered gun. The weapon had been concealed from view in a holster under his left armpit. Everett and Bristow staggered back in surprise as they heard its hammer being cocked. Colby raised the weapon and tried to aim at the man known as the Sunset Kid. The outlaw's crimson-covered finger jerked back on the trigger. An almighty blast spewed from the gun's barrel and sent a lump of lead hurtling at the bounty hunter. With the agility and speed of a mountain lion Sunset moved to the side as the bullet tore through the night air.

Sunset's hat was torn from his head and sent flying up into the air.

'That was a damn bad mistake ya made there, Hec,' Sunset drawled as he instinctively fanned his gun hammer twice. Ear splitting lead flamed from the barrel of his .45. Both bullets hit the outlaw in the throat. Gore erupted and sprayed in all directions from the ghastly wound.

Like a rag doll the lifeless figure crumpled in a heap into the already scarlet sand.

Clem was silent. He just stared at the body and then at the emotionless figure of the hunter of men.

Bristow waved the gunsmoke away and gazed open-mouthed at Sunset as he again spat at his latest victim.

'Ya can't just go killing critters, Sunset,' the sheriff raged with a wave of his fist.

'That's another two hundred bucks ya owes me, Sheriff.'

Before Bristow could say another word the defiant bounty hunter stepped over the body and turned towards the Diamond Pin saloon.

A thousand eyes watched the man as, walking

slowly, he slid the smoking Colt back into its holster and continued on until he reached the drinking hole.

Everett rubbed his mouth. It was dry. He had seen death many times but never had he seen anyone executed like that before. His thoughts drifted to Valko. His friend Valko was fast but could he match the speed of this creature?

'That critter is damn evil, Clem,' Bristow whispered.

'Reckon ya better arrange for the undertaker to collect this body, Chuck,' Clem said, his gaze following the bounty hunter.

'Yeah, reckon I'd best do that.' Bristow gave a nod and stared down at the twisted form lying between them. He did not say it but he was afraid. Afraid of a man who had just demonstrated how lethal he was.

Then Clem checked his gun.

'What ya intending doing, Clem?' the sheriff asked. 'Ya ain't thinking of going up against Johnny Sunset, are ya?'

'Not hardly,' the older man replied. 'I ain't suicidal, boy. But again, I sure ain't risking getting him fired-up without knowing my hogleg's loaded for bear.'

'Leave him be, Clem,' Bristow warned. 'He don't hanker for folks stepping on his toes.'

Clem Everett slid the gun back into its holster, smiled and then started to pace in the bounty hunter's tracks across the sand to the saloon where he had seen the deadly Sunset enter only a few seconds before. 'If'n ya hear a shot, come running, Chuck.'

Chuck Bristow felt his heart quicken inside his chest. He did not say another word as he watched his old mentor step up on to the boardwalk outside the Diamond Pin and push its swing doors apart. The sheriff shook his head, swung around to face the men and women hidden behind the store fronts and clapped his hands at a few of the burliest onlookers. Like a shepherd gathering a flock of reluctant sheep Bristow dramatically urged them forward to where the street's amber illumination danced across the pool of blood where he stood.

'C'mon, ya galoots. Git this damn carcass off the street.' He ordered. 'Take it down to the funeral parlour. C'mon.'

A few of the larger men reluctantly ventured from their hiding places and moved towards the body of Hec Colby. It was a gruesome sight even for those with guts made of iron.

'Pick him up,' Bristow demanded, clapping his hands. 'Don't go fretting none. It's only blood and blood can't hurt ya none.'

Four men leaned down and plucked the limp body off the sand and started to make their way towards the undertaker's office at the end of the long street.

Bristow followed the men and their cargo but kept looking at the doors of the Diamond Pin swinging on their hinges.

'Keep going. Blood can't hurt ya none,' the sheriff repeated before whispering under his breath: 'Unless it's ya own spitting out of bullet holes, that is.'

SIX

There was no mercy in the heart of the Shadow for he had managed to escape justice for so long that the thought of one day being held responsible for his atrocities no longer entered his head. He did what he wanted to do and dared the world to try and stop him.

The man disguised as the Valko Kid gave out a muted, yet sickening laugh as his rabid mind recalled how he had mingled with the people at the way station. Dressed in normal trail gear the Shadow had remained unnoticed whilst he listened to the innocent passengers and stagecoach crew. None of them knew what he was planning. None even suspected that the quiet man in their midst was about to add even more hideous crimes to the innocent Valko's already shattered reputation.

Nobody ever noticed the Shadow unless he was

dressed in black and claiming to be the youngster he secretly envied.

The Shadow strode out of the shack and mounted his waiting horse. He gave no thought to what lay behind him in the small wood-and-sod structure. All he could think about now was riding out to where the range ended and the smooth rounded boulders began. For the stagecoach would be arriving soon on its journey from the way station to Sioux City. The remote road cut through the maze of massive rocks and was the regular route used to transport those who had the price of a stagecoach ticket. Since its inception there had never been any trouble anywhere along the trail taken by the stagecoaches.

That was about to change.

The Shadow had plans. Plans which fermented inside his mind like a cancer. They could not be stopped, for the ferocious outlaw had no desire to stop.

He adjusted himself on his saddle and then stared down at the gunsmoke which trailed from the barrel of his holstered gun. A gun he had just used. The Shadow turned the disguised grey to face the distant moonlit rocks.

He checked his pocket watch and then gave a nod to himself.

'Reckon I got me about thirty minutes to get in place,' he told himself. 'Then I'll have me a whole heap of gold and a mighty pretty young gal to ransom for even more.'

The Shadow inhaled deeply. His mind returned to the two female passengers he had seen earlier at the way station. One appeared to be a paid companion for the far younger woman, who looked to be somewhere between childhood and adulthood.

The Shadow had listened intently to their every word. The two talkative females had given him more information than either of them knew. It did not pay to talk aloud when the Shadow was listening.

Soon they would both realize that naïve mistake.

He raised his black bandanna again and tied a firm knot at the nape of his neck. Although his face was virtually covered his deadly eyes were smiling.

Smiling as only the eyes of madmen can smile.

The Shadow gathered his reins and was about to spur when he heard the sound of an approaching horseman. The outlaw swung around on his saddle and saw a large weatherbeaten man seated astride a horse built for ploughing rather than riding.

'The second plate. I knew she had a man,' the Shadow muttered as he swiftly drew one of his guns and fanned its hammer. The deafening noise was only heard by one heartless creature.

The outlaw did not wait to see the lifeless body of the innocent man fall into the tall grass. The Shadow spurred and headed across the range of sweet grass towards the outcrop of smooth boulders and the road that he had already barricaded.

The horse had only just reached a canter when the lethal rider spotted the stagecoach making its way down through the rocks towards the road.

'Hell!' the Shadow cursed. 'The damn stage is early.'

He drove his spurs into the flesh of his mount.

Now it was a race against time. The Shadow had to reach the crude barricade before the stagecoach if he were to execute his plan perfectly. There was a lot at stake. A fortune in gold coin was one and another female was the other.

The horseman and the stagecoach were both roughly a mile away from the obstruction with which he had blocked the road. The grey horse thundered on across the range as its master's spurs continued to drive into its already bleeding flanks.

The rider would show his horse no mercy, just as he never showed people any mercy.

The swaying shoulder-high moonlit grass would hide his approach until he reached his goal, the horseman told himself.

The wide-eyed grey ploughed on through the high grass towards the road. It was not obeying its master but vainly trying to escape his relentless spurs.

SEVEN

The Diamond Pin was probably the largest of all the saloons in Sioux City. It stretched so far back that most of those who sat close to its swing doors could not see the rear wall for tobacco smoke and moving bodies. Fifty card tables filled the room as men drank and gambled, whilst females moved around trying to entice them up the wide elegant staircase to where a dozen bedrooms awaited.

An imported French chandelier hung on a brass chain from the oak-beamed ceiling roughly thirty feet into the saloon yet few of its patrons had ever noticed its existence unless they had been sprawled out, supine, looking upward. All that men desired when they entered any saloon was liquor and the company of a woman: any type of liquor and a certain type of woman. Both were plentiful in the Diamond Pin.

It was only a matter of minutes since the shooting had ended out in the street, but the saloon was back to business as usual. A horseshoe-shaped bar with five barkeeps kept the liquor flowing and the patrons happy. However, two men inside the saloon remained apart from the activities.

Neither had approached the bar; they sat at tables on either side of the large room.

Clem Everett sat alone, watching the bounty hunter through the haze of tobacco smoke, whilst Johnny Sunset watched everything and everyone with equal interest. He had spotted Clem as soon as the retired lawman entered the saloon. Sunset knew more about the ex-marshal than Everett could have imagined.

That was his job. He studied people because he knew that in order to remain alive in his profession you had to have knowledge of those around you. When you relied upon others you soon became another notch on someone else's gun grip.

Both men remained alone at their individual tables.

Soon they were watching only one another. Like a pair of stags waiting to prove their prowess they kept looking across the big room at each other.

The Sunset Kid seemed to be the only man whom the bar girls avoided and left alone. They went to everyone else, including Clem Everett, looking for trade but none of the girls ventured near the deadly bounty hunter.

It was if he had the scent of death upon him.

Each man was waiting for the other to do something: something that might give the other a reason to respond. They just stared with unblinking eyes. Eyes that burned across the distance that separated them, in anticipation of what might happen.

Although Clem Everett was by far the older of the pair and knew that he was no match for the lethal bounty hunter, he was somehow the calmer man.

He had lived too long amid the mindless violence of the West to be intimidated by anyone, however fast they were with their weapons. He had lived too long to be afraid of what might happen and had resolved long ago to fret only over what *was* happening. Clem knew that he was closer to the end of his life than most, and being so close had a way of making some men appear braver than they actually were.

After what seemed like an eternity in the busy and noisy saloon one of the men rose to his feet and approached other in determined strides. It was Johnny Sunset who had broken first. For all his superior ability with his two guns the bounty hunter had been unable to outstare the older man. Sunset strode towards Everett, and the crowd parted and silently watched.

The only person in the Diamond Pin who did not

appear to be either impressed or troubled was Clem Everett. It took more than a deadly bounty hunter to impress the seasoned lawman. Johnny Sunset had a confident swagger as he approached Everett but even that did not change the unworried look on the older man's face.

Sunset paused above the card table and looked down at Clem as he pulled the big gun from the holster on his right hip.

'What ya bin looking at me for, Everett?'

Clem raised an eyebrow and pushed his hat brim off his temple to look up into the bounty hunter's face more intently.

'So ya do know who I am, Kid,' Clem drawled.

Johnny Sunset dragged a chair away from the table and sat down upon it. He rested the distinctive weapon on the green baize and glared at it.

'Sure I know ya, Everett. I knew ya a long time back but you don't recall,' he said.

Clem rubbed his lip and studied the strange gun. 'Nope. I don't recall ever meeting you before, Kid. But when ya gets to live as long as I have ya do tend to forget most things, including gunslingers like you.'

'I ain't no gunslinger,' Sunset snarled.

'I was pitching ya a compliment.' Clem shrugged. 'Anyone as fast as you are ain't no normal bounty hunter. They're usually back-shooters. I'd bet my horse that you ain't never back-shot nobody.'

The Sunset Kid nodded. 'Dead right. Never needed to.'

Clem pointed at the big gun.

'Where'd ya find that cannon?'

'Had it made. Only one of its kind.'

'Ever use it?'

'Once,' Sunset answered. 'It blew two outlaws clean apart. There weren't enough left for me to claim the bounty on them.'

The retired lawman smiled.

'How'd ya know me, really?'

'I told ya,' Sunset replied. 'We met once.'

'Eyewash.'

Johnny Sunset smiled. 'Yep. But I heard tales about ya since ya hung up ya star. About what ya bin doing and who ya bin doing it with. Darn interesting and a tad confusing.'

Clem straighted up on his chair. 'Yeah?'

'Yep. I know a lot about you.'

'How?'

Sunset stood and picked up the large gun again. 'Well, I've bin trailing the Valko Kid for the last couple of months. The more I've learned about him the more I've learned about you.'

Clem also rose to his feet. 'Why'd you come to Sioux City? Of all the places to go, why'd ya choose this town?'

The bounty hunter stopped and stared down at

the sawdust-covered floor, then cocked one of the hammers on the unusual weapon. His head tilted slightly until his eyes were focused upon Everett. The retired lawman did not seem afraid of him or his rarely used gun: a wry smile crept across his face.

Suddenly Sunset swung on his heels, aimed the adapted scattergun at the impressive chandelier and fired. The huge blast rocked and deafened the entire room. A flash of raging buckshot spewed from one of the twin barrels, tore through the smoke-filled air and severed the chandelier's chain. The entire assemblage came crashing down. Men and women leapt to safety as a table was crushed beneath the weight of glass and metal. Candles flew in all directions.

Johnny Sunset laughed out loud at the sight of panicking men stomping on the fiery candles which were igniting the sawdust around the room.

'Reckon I'll have to pay for that demonstration but it was worth every penny, Everett,' the bounty hunter said. 'Nobody in his right mind would go up against this hunk of metal.'

Clem rubbed both his ears, stepped close to the bounty hunter and leaned into him. 'I asked ya a question, Kid. I want me an answer. Savvy?'

The bounty hunter holstered the smoking weapon. 'You know the answer to that'un, old-timer.'

Clem scratched his chin.

'I ain't too sure that I do, Kid. Enlighten me.'

'I told ya, I'm hunting Valko,' Johnny Sunset said again.

Clem glared at Johnny Sunset. He raised a hand and rested it on the younger man's shoulder. A gasp went through the saloon as men and women witnessed the act of either bravery or stupidity displayed by Everett.

'I'll ask ya again, Kid. How'd ya know the Valko Kid's headed here?' Clem asked.

Sunset looked at the lawman's hand upon his arm, then brushed it away before squaring up to the defiant Everett. If any other man had dared to touch him he would already have broken the man's jaw, but there was something about Everett which intrigued him.

'Ya must be plumb bored with living, old man.'

'Answer me, Kid,' Clem pressed. 'What brought ya here to Sioux City looking for the Valko Kid? What?'

Johnny Sunset sighed and leaned close enough for his whispered reply to be heard by only one person.

'Simple, Mr Everett. I was told that you were headed here. Where Everett goes ya sure to find Valko.'

The old marshal raised an eyebrow. 'What you implying, young'un?'

'I learned down in War Smoke about you and Valko.' Sunset sighed. 'I can't say I've figured it out

65

yet but for some reason you and that stinking outlaw seem to be buddies.'

'He's innocent, Sunset,' Clem said firmly. 'I'm just trying to help him prove it.'

'Innocent? Not in my book.' The bounty hunter headed for the bar counter and snapped his fingers at the nearest barkeep. As his boot rested on the brass rail Sunset turned around and looked at the ashen-faced Everett. 'To me he ain't nothing more than a real valuable outlaw I intend killing. If anyone tries to stop me I'll kill them as well, no matter what they used to be. There ain't nothing or no one gonna stop me collecting that twenty-five thousand dollars' reward money. Savvy, old-timer?'

Clem Everett inhaled long and deep, then gave a nod.

'Yep,' he drawled. 'I savvy.'

EIGHT

The dust-caked stagecoach came thundering through the moonlight and navigated the last of the massive boulders as its sweat-drenched driver cracked his reins and steered a course to reach the range. The road to the distant Sioux City was flanked on both sides by high swaying grass, allowing the deadly killer to ride unseen to where he had earlier barricaded the lonely road between the gigantic boulders.

The skilled driver elbowed the man riding shotgun gun beside him and pointed ahead of them at the brush and debris obstacle that blocked the road.

'Look!' the stunned driver yelled out over the sound of the galloping six-horse team. 'How in tarnation did that get there?'

The guard offered no suggestions. Both men knew

tumbleweed had a habit of being blown across the virtually flat range, thus hindering the progress of vehicles along the road's length, but neither man had seen quite so much debris before.

This time it had not been nature which had blocked the road, causing the stagecoach to stop. Unknown to the stagecoach crew, this was the work of the Shadow.

The six-horse team forged on beneath the bright moon towards the obstacle as both the stagecoach's driver and shotgun guard readied themselves to clear the road. Neither noticed the rider thundering through the shoulder-high grassland, on a course to intercept them.

The Shadow leaned over the neck of his horse and spurred mercilessly. The animal ploughed on through the tall grass, unseen by unwary eyes.

As the huge quantity of the debris that had been carefully placed across the road dawned on the stage-coach driver he jammed his stout boot down on the brake pole and hauled the reins up to his chest. The metal wheel rims screeched. Dust flew up from the leather brake pads as the coach slid from side to side on the rough ground whilst its team were brought to a halt.

Even so neither man suspected that the road had been deliberately blocked. Soon they would learn the truth. Fatally.

Close to the barricade in the high grass the Shadow dragged back on his reins, leapt to the ground and swiftly drew one of his guns. He cocked the hammer and dropped his reins. He was close to the barrier of debris, and he moved through the dark depths of the swaying shoulder-high grass towards the place where the stagecoach had come to rest.

The Shadow inhaled through the bandanna which masked his features. He could smell the perfume of his victims on the night air. The very perfume that he had inhaled back at the distant way station, where he had made his plans.

The merciless outlaw moved closer to the road. His eyes narrowed as they stared at the side of the vehicle. The stagecoach was now at a stop, yet dust still floated from beneath its wheels and the hoofs of its six-horse team.

The two men on the driver's board were arguing about who should climb down and remove the obstacle. Finally they seemed to agree that they would both clear the road.

The Shadow watched the pair of men slowly climb down to the road. The driver headed towards the pile of dried vegetation blocking the stagecoach's advance whilst the guard moved to the door of the carriage and opened it.

The ruthless outlaw silently made his way through the grass towards the vehicle as the guard stared into the interior of the coach at the pair of confused women.

'Sorry about the delay, ladies,' the guard said with a touch of his hat brim. 'We got us some brush blocking the road. Soon as we clear it we'll be on our way again.'

'It will be nice to be home again,' the older woman said.

'It sure will,' the younger woman agreed.

The guard smiled and then turned. Suddenly a gun barrel was thrust into his chest. It exploded into action. A flash lit up the shirt front of the guard. Both women screamed out hysterically as the blinding rod of lethal venom cut right through the guard.

The dead man stumbled and fell to the ground at the feet of the outlaw, who was clad entirely in black. The acrid stench of gunsmoke filled both passengers' nostrils as they gasped at the sight of the outlaw who presented himself in the open doorway of the coach.

The women were shaking and holding on to one another as the voice of the stagecoach driver called out.

'What in tarnation was that?'

With smoke still curling from his gun barrel the Shadow turned on his heels and fanned his gun hammer again. Once more a deafening rod of lightning erupted from the .45.

The Shadow grunted and glanced at the women. 'Don't fret. He ain't dead. I just winged him to make sure he does what I tell him to do.'

The terrified ladies clung together and stared in horror at the man with the black bandanna pulled up over his face. It did not muffle the suckening sound of his laughter.

'He'll be able to drive this coach on to the town yonder and deliver my note to the banker,' the Shadow told them.

'Note?' the older woman repeated the word.

'My father is the banker,' the young woman gasped.

'I know that,' the outlaw said.

Agnes Harper had tried to protect the younger woman for most of her life. Now, for the first time, she felt that all her efforts had been pointless.

'What note are you talking about?' she asked. 'Answer me, you animal!' she demanded.

The Shadow gave a slow nod. 'The ransom note to be delivered to the banker.'

'Ransom note?' the older woman stammered.

'Yep. The one for her pa, woman,' the Shadow snarled. 'Ain't you paying attention?'

Agnes Harper looked at the moonlit figure standing by the door and waved a small gloved fist at him. 'Are you intending take us hostage?'

'Nope. Only her.' The Shadow pointed his smoking

gun at the younger of the pair. 'You get to ride inside here all the way to town with my demands and tell her pa that she's bin kidnapped by the Valko Kid.'

'I will not allow it,' the feisty woman protested, wrapping her arms around her ward. 'I will not be parted from this sweet innocent child. Do you hear me?'

The Shadow jabbed her hard in her whalebone corset with his gun barrel.

'Listen up, ya old hag. You can ride inside here either alive or dead. I don't give a damn which it is. It's up to you.'

The elderly woman reluctantly gave a nod.

The Shadow grabbed the wrist of the fifteen-year-old Polly Wilson and hauled her out of the coach. She landed on her knees next to the dead shotgun guard and whimpered in terror.

'What you going to do to me?' Polly managed to ask as her captor pulled her back on to her feet.

The Shadow gazed at her.

He did not answer.

NINE

The haunting sounds of barking dogs echoed around the area of Sioux City where the darker souls of the sprawling town congregated. Each howl beckoned him deeper into the very bowels of the settlement, yet he did not hear their siren calls. Johnny Sunset moved through the back alleys of Sioux City until he found the livery stable close to the now empty stock pens. The big locomotive had long gone with its valuable cargo of whiteface steers filling its stock cars as the bounty hunter crossed the railroad tracks beneath the star-filled sky.

He was like a ghost when he wanted to be unseen by prying eyes. Sunset was a deadly killing machine who had never once failed to ensnare and dispatch his chosen target. Like a fighting cock he never quit until he had achieved his goal. There was no mercy in any part of his body. If the wanted posters said dead or alive, then he killed the outlaws with no more compassion than someone crushing a scorpion beneath his boot heel.

If the law proclaimed them unworthy of remaining alive the lethal bounty hunter was always happy to oblige, yet now for some reason which he could not fathom he was troubled. With each step he took his mind kept thinking of the words Clem Everett had spoken earlier in the Diamond Pin.

Why would a retired US marshal say that the infamous Valko Kid was innocent? It made no sense at all to the hardened hunter of outlaws.

Sunset followed his nose and made his way through the shadows towards where the majority of the town's horses were stabled. The tall building had seen better days and needed a fresh coat of paint but it served its purpose. There were three livery stables of various dimensions in the town. So far Sunset had visited two of them; now he was approaching what he had been told was the largest of them.

So far he had not found what he had been seeking.

The famed white stallion belonging to the wanted man known as Valko was not an animal that could be hidden easily, by all accounts. It was said to be the most powerful white stallion of its kind in the West, capable of a speed no other horse could match.

The bounty hunter had figured that if Valko was in

town, as he believed, the white stallion had to be near by. Sunset had learned many things about the outlaw and one of them was that he never allowed his mount to be far from him.

The intrepid horse had saved Valko's life many times by being able to outrun all those who challenged its might and pursued its master.

Johnny Sunset realized that most other outlaws would have swapped the distinctive animal for something less noticeable, to throw posses off his scent, but not the Valko Kid. He prized this horse above anything else because it was reliable. It was the reason the outlaw was still alive.

Yet the handsome stallion was both a blessing and a curse to its owner. As there were few other magnificent specimens of thoroughbred white stallions in the West, all who set eyes upon it knew who its master was.

Even so, Valko treasured the animal.

Johnny Sunset knew that this was the chink in the outlaw's armour: Valko's Achilles' heel. Sunset figured that if he could find the horse it would not be too tough to find its master. He aimed to find and kill the Valko Kid and claim the substantial bounty upon his head.

The first two livery stables had not had anything close to the horse he sought. Now he was facing the last of the town's stables. This was his final throw of the dice. If the stallion was not in there then Sunset would have to reconsider his plans.

There were fewer lights and far more shadows on this side of Sioux City, Sunset thought. This was the perfect place for someone who craved the cloak of night to shield them.

Sunset paused, then pulled out a long, thin cigar from his vest pocket. He gripped it between his teeth and struck a match as he considered the tall building before him. Smoke trailed from his lips as the bounty hunter walked towards it. There was no sound from the man who had long since quit wearing spurs when it became obvious that they betrayed him to those who were always on the lookout for individuals such as himself.

Sunset inhaled deeply on the cigar. He felt it filling his lungs as he paused beside the wide-open doors. The light of the stars and moon filtered through the uneven wooden planks that spanned its walls. The smell and sound of horses filled his ears and nostrils as he instinctively checked both his guns before advancing. His eyes darted around him, seeking more of the breed of men like Bearclaw Jacobs and Hec Colby. There seemed to be no one anywhere close by.

Johnny Sunset tossed the cigar away when he reached the large doors. His eyes narrowed as they penetrated the depths of the livery stable's interior.

Sparks floated upward from the blacksmith's forge in the very centre of the building. The forge still glowed but it was obvious it had not been used for several hours. Only the coals in the very middle of the forge were still red, yet their satanic light lit up everything round about.

The bounty hunter advanced into the gloom, then stopped.

'Ya looking for something, *amigo*?' a well-built man asked from a dark recess. The light of the glowing coals highlighted his seated muscular form.

Sunset did not answer straight away. He walked around the dirt floor and studied the horses in their stalls. Each of the animals studied him with equal interest. None of them was white, like the stallion he sought.

'Ya got a white stallion hid in here someplace?' the bounty hunter asked at last. 'I'm told it's a real big horse. A big powerful pure white stallion that looks like he could outrun any other four-legged critter on the face of the earth.'

'Nope.' The voice came back from the recess. 'If'n that's the kinda nag ya looking to buy then ya sure come to the wrong place, boy. All I got here is them critters ya looking at. Most is owned by locals like the sheriff and the like. Got me a few saddle horses over in the corner. I rents and sells them.'

Johnny Sunset brooded for a while, then moved

closer to the man who was sitting on a large box. A heavy leather apron hung from his neck and reached the floor.

'I didn't wanna buy it. I was just wondering if ya seen it, mister,' he explained. 'I am looking to buy some horseflesh, though.'

The man shook his head. 'I'm sure pleased ya don't wanna buy it seeing as I ain't got it to sell. Like I said, them nags over yonder are for sale.'

'Any of them fast?' Sunset asked. He screwed up his eyes and tried vainly to evaluate the horses. 'I'll be needing me a real fast'un.'

'One fast enough to catch this white stallion neither of us ever seen?' The man sounded amused as he rose to his feet.

Johnny Sunset studied the blacksmith. As was usual with his breed, he was a big man. He ambled to the side of Sunset and looked the bounty hunter up and down. He tutted as if disappointed, then made his way towards the horses.

'C'mon, weedy.'

Weedy? The bounty hunter trailed the huge man. Few men dared sass him and expect any prospect of living to tell the tale. Sunset gave dispensation to those who looked big enough to carry horses on their shoulders.

The liveryman paused and pointed at the last two stalls.

'Them two are said to be fast. Damned if I know if they are, though.' he said.

'I need the fastest one ya got,' Sunset told him. 'One that's got plenty of pace but also stamina.'

'The black with the diamond flame is kinda fast, I'm told. I rented him out a few times. Got a fair turn of speed and can keep going for hours. Leastways, that's what folks tell me. I never rode a horse in my life. They don't like men that's as heavy as I am on their backs.'

'I'll take it.' Sunset nodded. 'And I'll also need me a saddle and gear.'

The liveryman waved a hand at a wall covered in every sort of gear imaginable. 'I got everything ya need.'

Johnny Sunset considered the variety of saddles and harnesses. 'OK. You choose.'

'Ain't ya gonna haggle on a price?' The big man turned his head on his muscular neck and looked down at the bounty hunter. This time he was studying Sunset hard and with more interest. 'Everyone haggles.'

'I ain't got the time to waste.' Sunset knew he was being weighed up. 'What ya finding so interesting, big man?'

A finger on a powerful hand pointed at the unusual weapon in the right-hand holster of the bounty hunter.

'That's a mighty odd-looking shooting-iron ya got there, weedy,' the liveryman said. He raised his eyes to focus on the face of the Sunset Kid. 'Who the hell are ya?'

'My names's Johnny Sunset.'

'The bounty hunter?'

Sunset gave a nod. 'Yep.'

'When do ya want the horse?'

'Now.'

'That'll be two hundred dollars. Cash money.' The man was watching Sunset's face intently. There was no sign of emotion in it.

Sunset dipped two fingers into his pants pocket. 'Gold coin do ya?'

'Yep.' The large man nodded. 'Ya hunting some-body in Sioux City, Sunset?'

'Valko.' Sunset answered, pressing the coins into the large outstretched hand. 'I figured he'd be here by now but it looks as if I'll have to go hunting for the critter.'

'Is he the one that owns the white stallion?'

'So they say.' Johnny Sunset watched as the black-smith led the horse from its stall and ran a hand down its chest. It looked fast to the bounty hunter but the proof of that would be when it was put to the test.

The large liveryman scratched a match across his leather apron and lifted the glass bowl of a lantern

80

hanging from a nail close to the wall. He lit its wick and the interior of the large building was suddenly filled with a soft amber illumination. He set the lantern down carefully and stared at the bounty hunter.

'What ya gonna do when ya finds this Valko critter, Sunset?'

'Kill him,' the smaller man replied bluntly without hesitation. 'Kill him permanent. He's worth twenty-five thousand dollars.'

'I never even knew there was so much money in the whole world, young'un.' The blacksmith sighed. 'A man could live like a king with that sort of money.'

'Damn right.' Johnny Sunset approached the horse. It was skittish and shied from his outheld hand. 'Say, this horse is a tad nervous. I like that. It means he's smart enough to recognize trouble when it raises its head.'

The larger man nodded but his eyes were fixed upon the adapted shotgun which the bounty hunter had on his right hip. It looked to be a deadly and unforgiving weapon by any standards.

'So ya figuring on bringing Valko in dead, huh?'

Sunset almost grinned. 'Yep. Real dead.'

'I'd bet money on that. Reckon if'n ya gets close to that Valko Kid varmint and let loose with that cannon there ain't no way he'll survive.' The livery man tossed a blanket on the back of the black and patted it down. 'That gun could bring down a buffalo.'

Johnny Sunset nodded in agreement. 'Ya damn right.'

TEN

The night breeze cut across the vast range where thousands of cattle were congregated between a score of tiny shacks. With it a strange mist moved a few feet above the ground as frost was blown off the acres of swaying grass. The breeze was as sharp as the best honed of daggers. It cut into a person's bones no matter how much flesh they had covering them.

There was an eerie sound travelling with the mist which haunted the area beneath the vast canopy of stars and the bright moon. It was as though the gods themselves were trying to warn the innocent rider below of the deadly outlaw who was somewhere close.

Valko allowed the muscular mount to rest. He surveyed everything in the keen knowledge that death was never far from him. It waited unseen in a million places.

The Kid ran a hand across his face and sighed. He then turned and looked back. There was no sign of the posse that had dogged him for days. Jumping the ravine had proved to be his salvation for only men in fear of losing their lives ever attempted anything as foolhardy as that.

Wherever they were now it was sure that they would not find their prey this night, he told himself.

'You did good, Snow.' Valko patted the high-shouldered animal's neck. 'You saved my bacon again. Reckon I'll have to double your ration of feed.'

The white stallion snorted as if agreeing with its master.

Valko glanced down at the sand beneath his mount's front hoofs and noticed something. There were other horseshoe tracks leading away from the rise where he had stopped his horse. They led down to the range and the fertile grassland. A score of small shacks were dotted for as far as the eye could see but the tracks seemed to lead straight to the nearest of them.

'Looks like somebody else took this route, Snow,' the Kid said. He gripped the saddle horn and leant down to study the hoof marks. Then he straightened up and felt a icy chill trace his spine. It had nothing to do with the temperature. 'Damn it all. If I didn't know better I'd say them tracks was left by the same horse the Shadow rides. Leastways they're real similar.'

Valko pondered the thought for a few moments.

Could the man he had hunted for over a decade have left these tracks? Had he somehow accidentally stumbled on to the very thing he was seeking?

The Shadow?

Sweat trailed down his face from his hatband. Valko knew he was probably wrong but the thought kept gnawing at his innards.

He gathered up his reins in his hands and looked down to the small shack where he was convinced the hoof tracks led. As his eyes narrowed he could see that the only horse close to the hut was a barebacked monster of an animal. An animal bred to haul wagons.

Then his keen eyes spotted something close to the horse.

Something on the ground. It was bathed in the light which spilled out from the open door of the shack. The Kid stood in his stirrups and leaned over the neck of his horse.

'Damn.' Valko muttered as he realized it was a dead man. 'I thought I heard a gunshot earlier.'

Without a moment's hesitation Valko urged the horse on. The white stallion thundered down the rise and entered the expanse of tall grass which was between himself and the small shack. The horse obeyed its master as it always did.

Even without spurs Valko was able to get his faithful mount to obey his every command either by a flick of the reins or a verbal command.

The white stallion cleared the grass and came upon the open ground around the little shack. Again Valko saw the hoofmarks in the damp soil.

They led right up to the shack.

Valko drew rein. The stallion stopped close to the carthorse, which was standing over the dead body. The Kid looped a leg over his mount's head and neck and slid to the ground.

The smell of recently discharged gunsmoke lingered in the frosty air. Valko pulled one of his guns from its holster and cocked its hammer.

The lamplight was spread out across the churned-up ground outside the open door. Its amber glow highlighted the dead man as Valko reached him.

Every sense the youngster had in his survival arsenal told him that whoever had killed this man was gone. The Kid looked at the ground and could see where the horse had been turned and then spurred to ride from this place.

Valko screwed up his eyes and looked to where the horse had been ridden.

He focused on the huge rocks which rose up on the edge of the range.

'Now why would he head thataway?' the Kid vainly asked himself. 'Unless he intends hiding out for some reason.'

The distant lights of Sioux City caught his attention

for a moment and Valko thought about his old friend Clem. A friend who, he knew, would already be there waiting for his arrival.

'Sorry, pal. Reckon I'm going to be a tad late.' Valko swung on his heels. He was facing the open doorway with his gun held firmly in his grip at hip level. He knew that the killer was not inside the small ramshackle hut, but there might just be someone inside the shack with a weapon. A weapon ready to seek revenge upon anyone who made the error of being in the wrong place at the wrong time.

The youngster strode towards the shack.

The Kid could not hear anyone inside but still kept his gun ready just in case.

Valko reached the doorframe. He paused and looked inside for a brief moment before turning away and lowering his head. He felt sick. He had never seen anything quite so senseless before, but he knew who was responsible for the outrage. Only one evil creature did that to women, Valko thought. The man who masqueraded as him had left a trail of similar atrocities in his wake.

Valko rested his back against an upright and rammed his gun back into its holster.

'So it is you, Shadow,' the Kid mumbled angrily.

It had been many long years since Valko had been this close to the Shadow. He rubbed the tears from his eyes and tried to calm himself.

It was not easy.

Summoning all his resolve, Valko inhaled deeply and then ran to his horse. His left boot entered the stirrup as he grabbed hold of the saddle horn and swung his right leg over the hand-tooled saddle.

'C'mon, Snow. We got to catch that animal and put a stop to him ever doing this kinda thing again.'

The Valko Kid cracked his reins at the ground. The mighty white stallion responded like a cannon-ball being fired.

The stallion thundered on through the tall grass. The trail of Valko's foe was going to be easy to follow. The grass was beaten down where the Shadow's mount had previously torn through it on its way towards the unseen road.

The Valko Kid stood in his stirrups.

This time he would catch his prey, he vowed.

This time he would put an end to the slaughter by putting an end to the Shadow.

ELEVEN

Johnny Sunset looked at the readied mount and gave a satisfied nod of his head. He said nothing as he took the reins from the beefy hands of the black-smith and led the horse out into the darkness where only a few scattered lanterns gave any clue to there being life in this part of Sioux City. He ran a hand down the neck of the nervous creature before reaching up to the saddle horn. He was about to take hold of it when he heard a noise across the a street. A familiar noise.

The skilled bounty hunter lowered his arm again and rested it on the holstered .45 as he moved the horse between himself and the unnerving sound. Sunset licked his dry lips and looked over the saddle. He peered into the depths of the shadows.

Only the railtracks seemed alive as the high moon shimmered over them. Sunset held the horse in check and kept it between himself and the noise, which was growing louder.

Spurs, he thought. Spurs moving towards him.

Sunset heard the large blacksmith moving behind him but did not turn. His eyes remained glued to the shadows, waiting for a glimpse of whoever it was out there. Whoever it was walking toward the livery stable.

'I'd stay inside if I was you, friend,' Sunset advised.

'What's wrong, Kid?' the blacksmith asked. With his shovel-sized hands he started to close the high doors behind the bounty hunter. 'You scared of something?'

'I ain't never been scared of nothing, friend,' Sunset replied in a low rasping tone. A tone which was designed for the ears of only one man.

'You sure looks scared,' the blacksmith gruffed.

'There's somebody out there,' Sunset said. 'Somebody headed this way. Hear them spurs?'

The blacksmith paused. 'If you ain't scared then how come you ain't mounted that nag? How come you're using it like a damn shield?'

'Listen up. I've already had two varmints try and kill me in the last hour, friend. I ain't hankering for a third.' Sunset screwed up his eyes. He could vaguely see the tall figure moving towards him through the blackness.

'Maybe that's the Valko Kid, Sunset.' The black-smith chuckled. 'I reckon he's come looking for the *hombre* that's looking for him. I can't see no big white horse, though.'

Exasperated Sunset turned his head and glanced at the amused character. 'Will you shut the hell up?'

'There he is.' The blacksmith pointed.

'I see him.' Sunset exhaled a long breath.

The figure cleared the furthest of the shadows and then stopped walking. He was tall. Real tall. He was also carrying a cocked carbine across his waist, partly hidden by the tail of a poncho.

'I see ya, Sunset,' the man bathed in blackness called out at the bounty hunter. 'I see ya hiding behind that lump of glue.'

The blacksmith sniffed and then bellowed out. 'Don't you go calling my horse a lump of glue. That's prime horseflesh there and make no mistake about it.'

Johnny Sunset spat at the ground as he pulled his .45 free of its holster and cocked its hammer. 'I told you to hush the hell up, friend. That critter's just trying to rile me up. He's looking for a clear target.'

The blacksmith raised his voice at Sunset. 'You better be ready to pay extra if my horse gets shot up, boy. You hear?'

The strange figure raised his head and stared at the man still partly hidden by the handsome horse.

'Will you two stop gabbing like a pair of old prairie hens? I asked me some questions up on Main Street,

Sunset,' the man said before he resumed his approach. 'I was told you killed my old pard Hec Colby. I don't cotton to folks that go around killing my pals. Why's ya kill him?'

Sunset knew that even he could not simply kill someone without there being a reason. He wondered if the loud-mouthed man might be wanted like his dead friend. Sunset's eyes strained as they tried to make out who it was heading straight at him.

'Why? Hell! He was wanted dead or alive, stranger,' Sunset yelled over the top of his saddle. 'Who might you be?'

'I'm Hec's pard,' came the unhelpful reply.

Suddenly the glow of a lonely lantern hanging from a porch roof spilled its light over the tall man. His face was lit up and suddenly the bounty hunter recognized him.

'Denver Creek,' Sunset shouted out. 'Is that you, Denver?'

The outlaw stopped. 'It sure is, Sunset.'

'That's all I wanted to know.'

Johnny Sunset threw himself away from the mount he had only just paid dearly for and hit the ground rolling. As he rolled he cocked and fired. Three deadly bullets cut across the darkness and hit the wanted man dead centre before the bounty hunter came to a rest.

Creek wavered for a while, then dropped his

unused rifle as death overwhelmed him. Sunset had risen and started towards him before the outlaw had dropped on to his knees.

There was a look of total surprise on the outlaw's face. Three bullet holes were spilling gore through his poncho.

'What ya go do that for?' Creek asked as his fingers vainly clawed at the gun on his hip. A gun he could not draw.

Johnny Sunset reached down, pulled the gun from its holster and tossed it aside. He stared at his lethal handiwork and wondered why Creek had not managed to die yet.

'You happen to be worth five hundred dollars, Denver,' Sunset answered.

'Oh.' Creek closed his eyes, then toppled forward on to his face. He did not feel his nose breaking as it collided with the metal rail track.

The Grim Reaper had already claimed him.

TWELVE

The strange aroma inside the funeral parlour was unlike any scent found anywhere else, and neither Bristow nor Clem cared much for it. There were two dead bodies inside the small building, freshly washed. The sound of hammering was coming from the back room as the undertaker's assistant busied himself in making two coffins from spare timber. Outlaws never warranted anything grander than a crude rectangular box of pine.

The sheriff headed out into the street seeking fresh air and to take time for the cool night air to refresh his weary mind. Everett followed and gave out a long sigh as he closed the door behind him. Then he ambled to the edge of the boardwalk and stared down at his reflection in the water trough.

Bristow ran a match across his belt buckle, cupped its flame over his pipe bowl and sucked hard until a cloud of smoke surrounded his head.

'Sunset sure don't waste no time, Clem,' the sheriff observed between puffs. 'He likes killing and that kinda troubles me. I never could see why some folks just gotta kill all the time. Hell. Life ain't long enough at the best of times, so why run the risk of it shortening? Don't ya agree?'

Clem raised a boot, placed it on the rim of the trough and nodded thoughtfully. 'Yep. It is a mite troubling. Johnny Sunset hankers for sending folks to Boot Hill. Reckon he never once even thought that some of them outlaws could be a better shot than him. Troubling, OK.'

Bristow tossed the spent match aside and edged closer to his old boss. He knew that something was gnawing at the tall man's craw. Something Everett seemed unable to tell his old pal about.

'You OK? Ya seem kinda quiet. I never seen ya like that in the old days, Clem. Dead 'uns never bothered ya before.'

Clem stared at his friend but all he could think about was another friend. One whom he feared would also end up inside the funeral parlour if he turned up in Sioux City whilst Johnny Sunset was in town.

'Them dead folks don't trouble me none, boy,' Clem said. He rested a hand on his raised knee.

'Is it that stinking bounty hunter that's chewing at

ya craw, old-timer?' Bristow kept puffing and blowing lines of smoke at the ground as the town appeared to be getting even busier than usual. 'Ya looked as white as a ghost when ya come from the Diamond Pin a while back. What happened in there, Clem? Did Sunset threaten ya or something?'

'Nothing really happened, Chuck.' Clem lowered his leg back to the boardwalk and rested his hands on his gun grips. 'Me and Sunset had us a little confab and he showed me how good that cannon he's got works.'

'So ya got on like ya was the best of friends, huh?'

Clem nodded. 'Bosom buddies.'

'Don't go giving me that spittle, Clem,' Bristow said. They started to walk back along the boardwalk in the direction of the sheriff's office. 'I've known ya for the better part of my life and I can tell when ya all fired up or just troubled. Something ain't sitting right with ya. What is it?'

Clem inhaled long and hard. He knew that the Valko Kid might show up at any time and although his pal would never guess who he was, there was no way that Johnny Sunset would not recognize the man on the powerful white stallion.

'I got something I have to tell ya, Chuck,' Clem at last managed to admit.

'I know that.' Bristow puffed. 'I've bin waiting for a long time for ya to tell me.'

They crossed the busy street and stepped up on the boardwalk outside an aromatic café. They paused to inhale the scent of cooking steaks and fresh-brewed coffee.

Everett looked into the virtually empty café. 'C'mon. I'll buy ya a cup of coffee that ya can actually drink without chewing.'

The lawman laughed and trailed Everett into the small café. Bristow waited for his old superior to remove his hat and sit down before he lowered his own wide rump on to a chair next to Everett. He removed the pipe stem from his teeth and scowled at Clem.

'It's like pulling teeth waiting for you to tell me things.'

Clem looked into the man's eyes. Eyes which were now wrinkled and baggy like his own. He smiled.

'Sorry, pal. This is hard for me. I don't want ya to lose any respect ya might have for this old man. I ain't got a whole lot left but the respect of old pals like you.'

Bristow tapped the pipe bowl on the chair leg and then pushed the pipe into his vest pocket. He rested an elbow on the chequered table cloth and studied his friend.

'This is serious, ain't it?'

Clem nodded. 'Yep.'

Bristow rubbed his whiskered jaw. 'Something to

do with Johnny Sunset and him wanting to kill Valko, I'll wager.'

Everett slowly nodded again. 'Yep.'

'Why would that bother Clem Everett?' the sheriff asked aloud. He thought for a moment and leaned back on his chair before pointing a knowing finger at the retired lawman. 'You gotta know this Valko critter. Know him better than ya ought to do. Right? Sunset wanting to kill him is burning ya up. Am I right?'

Again Clem nodded. 'Yep. Ya right, young'un.'

The sheriff dragged his hat from his head and slammed it on to the table between them. 'I am?'

'Ya hit the nail on the head, boy.' Clem sighed heavily.

Bristow leaned across the table. 'Are ya loco? Ya knows a stinking outlaw and ya worried that he'll get himself killed by a bounty hunter? Has ya lost the few beans ya had in that old head of yours? We don't make friends of stinking outlaws, Clem. It just ain't done.'

'Ain't as simple as that, Chuck.'

'But however much we hate the guts of bounty hunters they're on the same side as us,' the sheriff insisted. 'Hell, we rode in posses together for years hunting down outlaws and now ya on the side of one of them outlaws? Maybe the worst outlaw of them all if'n his price tag is anything to go by.'

Clem Everett could do nothing but listen to the words from his old deputy and know that there was no rational argument to be made. He had hunted Valko himself for years and come close to killing the young man on several occasions. All that had changed, though, when he had encountered the mysterious creature who disguised himself as Valko. Even then Clem had not been totally convinced until the wronged Valko had saved the life of the marshal who had tried so determinedly to end his own existence.

The image of the face owned by the Shadow still haunted Everett. He had looked down the barrel of one of that man's guns and tasted its lead. He had seen how the true Valko Kid had virtually lost his own life in an attempt to send the unscrupulous Shadow fleeing.

It was then that Marshal Clem Everett had realized that he had been hunting the wrong man. He owed Valko his very life and that was a debt he knew he could never repay. From that moment on Clem had vowed to try and clear the youngster's name. Months had become years and still the sword of Damocles had remained hanging above Valko's head.

Only the capture of the impostor would end the years of injustice for the man known as the Valko Kid. Only the capture or death of the Shadow could achieve that goal.

'Ya wrong, Chuck,' Clem said in a low whisper.

'About what, Clem?'

Everett stirred the cup of black coffee which had been placed before him by the buxom woman who either owned the small café or just worked there.

'About Valko,' Clem added as he watched the woman return to her kitchen.

The sheriff rested both elbows down on either side of his own cup of black beverage and squinted in the lantern light at the face of his old boss. Everett was grey now. His hair and his skin had virtually no colour apart from the brown spots caused by years of riding beneath a hot sun.

'Folks don't get bounties as high as Valko's unless they're real bad varmints, Clem,' Bristow said. 'Hell. You taught me that when I was a snot-nosed runt.'

The hooded eyes of the older man looked across the table.

'I taught ya wrong, boy. Valko ain't done none of the bad things he's branded as having done. Not one of them.'

Bristow eased back on his chair. He did not speak as he took in the short statement. Everett had never admitted to being wrong in all the years he had known him. It did not sit well with the sheriff.

'He's due here at any time, ain't he?' the sheriff asked.

Clem nodded. 'Yep. I'd appreciate it if'n ya could

turn a blind eye for the sake of an old friend, Chuck. Valko will have enough on his plate with Sunset.'

'Unlike you, I ain't loco.' Bristow sighed. 'I ain't gonna get in between them two varmints.'

Then before any more words were uttered between them the frantic sounds of mayhem erupted out in the street once more. A few horsemen raced past the open door of the café as men on foot looked and pointed at something at the far end of Main Street. The sound of a gun being fired echoed all around the small café.

'Sunset?' Bristow posed the name as though it were a question.

'I don't think so. I can hear a stagecoach,' Clem said and rose to his feet. He looked at the people and saw their reactions to the noise out in the street. 'Someone is in trouble. C'mon.'

The two men hurried out of the small café. Both stood among the crowd under the porch overhang on the boardwalk and squinted through the amber lantern-light along the street. The noise of an approaching stagecoach grew louder. More shots rang out.

The shots lit up the dark sky as their fiery lead went heavenward. Somewhere down near the very end of the street the familiar rattling of chains and snorting horses grew even more distinct.

'Reckon that's a stage,' Clem said confidently as he

pushed men and women aside to reach his horse still tethered outside the sheriff's office. Clem pulled his rope from his saddle horn and started to unwind it to make a lasso. 'A stage in trouble.'

'What ya figuring on doing, Clem?'

'Stopping it,' Clem retorted. 'What else?'

Bristow watched the older man leap down into the street and start to swing the rope over his head as the crowd parted and the stagecoach suddenly appeared. The snorting horses were white-eyed and terrified as the wounded driver sat helplessly on his perilous perch with a smoking .45 in his hand. The team were out of control and their long reins dragged beneath the belly of the vehicle.

Another shot went heavenward from the gun in the driver's hand as the wounded man slumped over on to his side.

Everett spun and threw the rope. He sent the lasso across the heads of the two lead horses, then dug his heels into the ground and hauled in the opposite direction. The noose tightened. With the rope looped around his shoulder and waist Everett was pulled violently off his feet and flew through the air before he landed on the soft sand twenty feet away. The team of six lathered-up horses came to a reluctant halt after dragging Clem another fifty feet down the street.

Sheriff Bristow ran to his friend and helped him

back to his feet. He brushed him down.

'Ya are loco,' Bristow said. 'Plumb loco. Ya could have broke ya neck.'

'Stop gabbing and check out them horses, boy,' Everett growled. He dropped the rope and started towards where he could see the driver slumped. 'I reckon they could spook again.'

Clem staggered to stand below the driver's seat. He had no sooner stopped than the blood-soaked driver fell from his high perch.

Somehow Clem caught the man before he hit the ground. Using every last remaining drop of his strength Clem eased him to the sand.

'What happened here?' Clem asked the half-dead man.

The driver's eyes flickered and he gave out a long sigh as his bloodstained hands gripped Everett's arm. 'We was held up. Charlie was killed. Just after we cleared Bodine Rocks.'

'Was Charlie the guard?' Clem pressed as Bristow reached his side and looked down at the horrific sight.

The driver gave a croak and a nod and raised one of his hands. It had been savaged by the rough. leather reins he had fought with on his journey to town.

'An outlaw come from nowhere. The road was blocked and we had to stop. When we got down to clear it Charlie was cut in half by an outlaw's bullet. Honest, I never even seen where the bastard come from. He shot Charlie and then plugged me. He spared me to bring the stage on in to town.'

Clem looked at Chuck. 'That don't seem logical.'

'It sure don't,' Bristow said. He looked down at the driver. 'Ya a lucky man, Pete.'

The driver shook his head and repeated. 'No I ain't, Chuck. He never meant to kill me. I was saved to bring the damn stage here. I heard him telling the passengers. Didn't make no sense at all.'

Bristow leaned over. 'What? Why'd he want ya to do that?'

Then the door handle of the carriage creaked and the dust-covered door opened. A woman in blood-splattered finery ventured out. A very shaken Agnes Harper had arrived home but without her ward. She had been thrown around within the confines of the stagecoach like a rag doll. Cuts covered her face.

'Sheriff. Sheriff,' she called out.

The sheriff moved to her and helped her to disembark, shaking, from the carriage. She wrapped her arms around the man with the tin star and sobbed hysterically.

'Easy there, Miss Harper. Ya safe now. Everything will be OK now. Ya home.'

The woman gripped the lawman's shoulders and looked up into his face. Tears raced down her cheeks and mingled with the blood.

'Y-you don't understand, Sheriff. He's got young Polly.'

Clem got back to his feet as others gathered around the wounded driver. He moved close to Bristow and the woman who gripped his shoulders so feverishly. He said nothing but listened to every word.

'Ya got to do something, Sheriff,' the woman implored.

'Who got Polly, Miss Harper?' Bristow asked firmly.

Agnes Harper burst into even more tears when she spied her employer across the street as he left the stage depot and began the long walk towards them. Rufe Wilson was the owner of the town's only bank and the widowered father of the innocent Polly. As was his ritual he had come to meet his daughter and the woman who was her constant companion.

'What's going on?' Wilson called out.

The sheriff shook Anges Harper until he regained her attention. 'Calm down, Miss Harper. Tell me. Tell me who got little Polly?'

She looked straight into his eyes.

'The outlaw,' she stammered before she added: 'The Valko Kid got Polly.'

The stunned sheriff looked over her head straight at Clem and shook his head.

'The Valko Kid,' he repeated angrily. 'I should

have known.'

Clem Everett said nothing. He turned and walked away from the scene. He was thirsty. This time he required something stronger than coffee.

THIRTEEN

Sheriff Bristow watched in stunned awe as the crowd around him moved like an ocean trying to find a beach. He leaned over and helped the stagecoach driver back to his feet, then allowed the men who surrounded them to take the wounded man in the direction of the doctor's house. A few whiskey-filled men remained around the lawman as Bristow kept rubbing his unshaven jaw.

'What ya thinking about, Sheriff?' one asked.

'You considering forming a posse?' another chipped in.

Bristow nodded furiously. His eyes remained on the saloon, into which he had watched his old mentor disappear to drown his sorrow.

'Well, Sheriff?' yet another swaying cowboy asked.

'Yep.' Bristow confirmed as he smashed a fist into the palm of his left hand. 'I'm going to form a posse, boys. A damn big'un. We got us a black-clad skunk to catch and kill and his name's Valko. The Valko Kid.'

There was a chorus of grunts from the men who surrounded Bristow. There was nothing better than hunting and killing a man when your guts were filled with rotgut rye.

'How come you still looks like you bin sucking on a cactus, Sheriff?' a wrangler with half-closed eyes somehow observed.

Chuck Bristow raised a hand and pointed at the Diamond Pin angrily. He sucked in air and then glanced at each man in turn before snarling:

'Why do I look so like I swallowed me some water from a bad well?' the sheriff snorted. 'I'll tell you boys why. I just seen me the best lawman I've ever known walk with his tail tucked between his legs into that saloon. For the last half-hour my oldest pal has bin bending my ear about a certain Valko Kid. Telling me that the critter was a good little boy and not the murderous bastard his Wanted poster reckons he is. The truth sure hurts and my old pal is hurting.'

'We still making a posse, Sheriff?'

'Yep.' Then Bristow growled at the nearest cowboy, 'Go get us a string of fresh horses from the livery. The rest of you come with me to my office. I'll dish out carbines and ammunition.'

FOURTEEN

The range was quiet apart from the sound of the breeze which swept across it and the thundering of the white stallion's hoofs as they ate up the ground between the small shack and the trail that led from Bodine Rocks to Sioux City. Yet the strange, eerie light of the bright moon could not hide the hideous reality which lay on the old road carved out through the sea of grass. It was a story of merciless slaughter. Steam still rose from the body which lay in the pool of its own blood. The gore had spread out in a circle around the hapless shotgun guard's corpse, brutal evidence of what had only recently occurred.

Standing high in his stirrups Valko could see the dead man long before he reached the dusty road. If evidence were required that this had been done by the evil Shadow it was there lying in that pool of gore. Blood sparkled upon the frosty ground as the mighty white horse approached.

'Easy, Snow,' Valko commanded his mount as the snorting animal sensed the death in front of them. 'Reckon we now know what the shooting was that we heard.'

The Kid stopped the muscular horse and lowered himself down on to his saddle. He looped the reins around his saddle horn and stared down from his lofty perch at the scene. Even the night could not disguise the senseless slaughter from the young horseman.

Once again Valko knew that yet another murder would be added to the long tally pinned to his name.

Valko dismounted swiftly and walked towards what was left of the dead shotgun guard. The light of every star in the sky as well as the brilliant moon reflected into his eyes from the wide circle of glistening blood.

The Kid paused and looked around him. The Shadow had gone but the youngster knew he still had to be close. Mighty close.

The frost-covered road held the clues to which direction the murderous creature had taken. The ground was scarred by the hoofs of the Shadow's mount. Valko studied it and then stared at the huge rounded boulders about a half-mile behind him.

'Hide like the vermin you are, Shadow,' Valko muttered as his eyes squinted at the moonlit rock before vowing: 'There ain't no place safe for you now. Not this time. I've got your scent and I ain't quitting until I get my hands on you. You're gonna pay this time. Pay for every damn thing you've ever done to the innocent folks you've hurt and killed.'

The white stallion snorted and walked towards its master, then scraped at the ground with one of its hoofs. Valko turned his head and looked at the horse.

'What's the matter, Snow?' he asked.

Again the stallion scraped the ground.

The Kid moved away from the body and then spotted something close to the edge of the road, half-hidden by the sweet grass. It was the strongbox from the stagecoach.

'Damn! Ya got good eyesight,' Valko told his mount. He knelt and looked at the metal box. Its lid had been forced open by a well-aimed bullet which had shattered its padlock. Valko moved the papers around but could not find any money. 'So the evil bastard managed to clean this thing out, but I ain't convinced that this is why he held up the stage. There gotta be another reason for him to risk his neck.'

Valko raised himself back up to his full height.

A million questions flashed through his young mind.

After chasing this man for so many years Valko had come to suppose that he knew how the Shadow thought.

What was the purpose of this hold-up?

The stallion snorted again and walked across the road to the opposite side. Valko trailed the intelligent creature and then saw what had attracted the white horse like a moth to a flame.

Caught high on the tall grass there was a small fragment of white cloth fluttering like a tiny flag. The Kid reached it and plucked it free.

He then turned it to face the moon and its helpful illumination.

This was no normal innocent scrap of cloth, Valko told himself as he studied it carefully. This was silk. Boasting embroidery at its finest and most costly.

A silk handkerchief with the initials P.W.

The faintest whiff of scent caught Valko's nostrils.

Valko raised the scrap to his nose and inhaled its perfume.

The sort of perfume favoured by young females, he told himself. With no hesitation the Kid pushed the delicate cloth into his shirt pocket.

That was it, his mind told him.

That was the answer.

The Shadow had been lured to the stagecoach by a woman or even women. Valko knew that a mere strongbox was not enough to make the evil creature strike, no matter how much money it held.

But a handsome woman could do it.

The Shadow was a slave to his own depravity.

Again the young man stared down at the ground, then saw the tell tale signs of a woman's footprints in and around the pool of blood. Two sets of slightly differing shoe shapes.

The Kid thought aloud: 'There were two of them. Two women. There ain't no sign of the Shadow bringing a spare horse so he must have only taken one of them with him to them rocks. His horse could manage that.'

Valko then saw the wheel-rim tracks which led from the bloody mess on the ground. 'And he let the stage go on to town. That must be why he never killed the driver as well. The other woman must have gone back inside the coach.'

The horse moved to the side of the young Valko and nudged its master in the back. 'Why'd he let them go and not the shotgun guard, boy?' Valko said, 'That don't figure.'

It was another question impossible to answer.

The Kid patted the neck of his magnificent stallion, stepped in his stirrup and mounted. He turned the horse and stared at the smooth moonlit rocks. They beckoned him. The Valko Kid knew that the bright moonlight was no protection against the deadly guns of the Shadow, but there was no choice. He had to follow even if it meant riding to his own death. Valko glanced over his broad shoulder back at Sioux City. The settlement stood out in the darkness like a swarm of fireflies as a myriad lantern lights defied the night. Then, as the Kid wrapped the reins around his right wrist, he gave a fleeting thought to his old pal Clem Everett and the appointment he might never be able to keep.

Wistfully the Kid touched the brim of his black Stetson as if in salute to the friend he knew would be there vainly waiting for his arrival.

'Sorry, Clem. I got me some unfinished business to try and settle,' he whispered into the cutting night air.

Then he heard a noise. A noise that chilled Valko even more than the cold air. It was the sound of a woman screaming somewhere in the maze of rocks. His heart raced.

So there *was* a woman out there, Valko thought. He had been right in his reading of the clues that lay around him. The Shadow had taken one of the women, just as he had suspected.

Valko raised himself up in his stirrups and balanced as another pitiful cry echoed from the distant boulders.

Vainly his keen eyes searched for her. He swallowed hard and swung the stallion around as he tried to see how many ways there were up into the cluster of rocks. There was only one route in and out.

'C'mon, Snow. We got us a gal to save and a varmint to catch,' Valko said. 'Go, boy. Go fast.'

The horse snorted and sprang powerfully into action beneath its young master.

The heroic horseman remained standing in his stirrups and allowed his mount its head. Like a white phantom the stallion thundered along the dusty road towards the boulders as yet another scream filled the range.

With each stride of his magnificent mount a single thought kept gnawing at the young rider's mind. If he could capture the Shadow and take him to Sioux City he might be able to prove his innocence once and for all.

The thought drove him on.

On towards what he knew might turn out to be his own death.

The white horse galloped towards the great boulders. Soon the sound of his horse's hoofs would be echoing off the rock.

All that protected Valko as he rode into six-shooter range was his own courage.

It was his only shield.

FIFTEEN

Clem Everett placed the empty whiskey glass down on bar counter, gave a knowing nod at the nearest bartender and wiped his mouth across his jacket sleeve. The bartender obliged and refilled the small thimble glass with another shot of the powerful liquor.

'So you was a marshal a while back, I hear?' the bartender remarked. He remained holding the half-empty whiskey bottle ready for action. 'I'd have liked to have bin a lawman but I got me enough folks shooting at me in this job. Hell. I reckon wearing a star would be worse.'

'Yep.' Clem Everett gave a thoughtful nod of his head and downed his second glass of fiery liquid. He pushed the glass forward once more with two fingers of his left hand. The retired lawman had a lot on his mind and was not inclined to enter into smalltalk

116

with a stranger no matter how much rye he had in his bottle.

Clem's mind raced. He was still unable to fathom what had occurred out there on the moonlit range.

The respectable-looking Agnes Harper had been adamant that her ward had been snatched by the Valko Kid after he had slain the stagecoach guard. She was also entirely convinced that their assailant *had* been Valko.

Why had she been so convinced?

How could a respectable lady know who the Valko Kid was or what he looked like?

Suddenly, as the third glass was pushed toward Clem's awaiting hand the answer came crashing into his tired mind. Agnes Harper had been told by the killer that his name was Valko. It was the only explanation. He had *told* her he was the Valko Kid.

There was only one man who would do that. The man who had been doing that very same thing for more than ten long years in order that all his crimes should be placed on another man's shoulders.

'The Shadow!' Clem banged his clenched fist on the damp bar counter.

'What you say, old-timer?' the barkeep asked.

Clem glanced at the man and then pushed the glass back. 'I don't need any more whiskey, pal.'

'Something troubling you, old-timer?' the barkeep asked. Clem glanced at the man with the hovering whiskey bottle in his hand.

'Not any more,' Clem replied. He tossed a coin at the confused man with the drooping moustache.

'That'uns on me,' Clem said. Then he turned to face the swing doors.

'Ain't ya gonna drink it?' the bartender asked.

Clem paused, then glanced back. 'Nope. I've had my fill. I got me something to do. Something mighty important, boy.'

'Good luck, old-timer.' The bartender lifted the glass and swallowed its contents. He watched Everett continue on his way towards the lantern-lit street. 'Something tells me you're gonna need it.'

The fresh air felt good. It woke a man up and sharpened his wits. Clem rested both wrists on his gun grips and looked to where the stagecoach and its exhausted team were still attracting a crowd. He adjusted his hat and focused on the horse on which he had seen Johnny Sunset mounted.

It was tied up outside the hardware store, just beyond his own mount outside the sheriff's office. A wry smile crept over the wrinkled features of the retired lawman.

'Reckon I know how to slow that bounty hunter up a tad.' Clem said to himself. He began to walk along the boardwalk towards the tethered horse. 'Give myself a chance of finding Valko before he does.'

The plan was simple, as most good ones are.

He pulled out a folding knife from his pants pocket and opened its blade. The blade, like its owner, had seen better days but both were sharp enough to handle the plan that had hatched inside Clem's brain.

The interior of the sheriff's office was noisy as his old deputy Chuck Bristow handed out rifles and boxes of ammunition to his hastily assembled posse.

None of them noticed as Clem pulled his reins free of the hitching rail and continued on to the hardware store and the bounty hunter's saddle horse.

Clem paused between the two animals and stared through the large window at the deadly hunter of men. Sunset was making a big show of purchasing enough ammunition for his arsenal of lethal weaponry.

Then, faster than the blink of an eye, the retired lawman reached down and slid his knife blade across the cinch strap, severing it.

'That'll slow you up, Johnny Sunset,' Clem said, folding his knife up once more. 'Now you'll have to find yourself a new saddle before you can hunt my pal.'

Clem pocketed the knife in his pants and took hold of his saddle horn. He stepped into his stirrup and eased his aching bones up on to the saddle. His gloved hands gathered up his reins and he turned his horse.

As he sat high on his saddle Clem noticed the woman who had been in the stagecoach rushing to the sheriff's office, accompanied by an alarmed-looking man. A man who had just learned that his daughter had been kidnapped and was being held for ransom. A man carrying a canvas bag swollen with money.

The horseman raised a hand and stopped both of them in their tracks. He gave a respectful nod to Agnes Harper.

'What's happening, ma'am?' Clem asked.

'This is my employer Mr Wilson,' the woman replied.

'Your ex-employer, Agnes,' Wilson corrected. He stared up at the mounted figure. 'And who might you be?'

'I ain't nobody special,' Clem answered.

'Then get out of my way, you old fool,' Wilson snapped. 'I have to deliver a ransom to the bastard who abducted my precious daughter. Come on, Agnes. We have to find Bristow.'

They continued on their way.

Clem touched his hat brim at the departing pair and watched them enter the sheriff's office.

Clem turned his mount and navigated a course through the array of people and vehicles. Then he spurred.

Nobody noticed the departure of the elderly horseman.

SIXTEEN

The moon made a terrifying companion to the aged Clem Everett as he forced his horse on towards the distant and ominous boulders that faced him. The eerie light of the bright moon made everything appear to be bathed in a blue hue. The veteran horseman kept on spurring feverishly in order to put as much distance as he could between himself and the deadly Johnny Sunset. He glanced over his shoulder. There was still no sign of the bounty hunter, he thought.

There was still a chance he might find his old pal to warn him before Johnny Sunset caught up with him.

'Keep going, boy,' Clem yelled into the pricked ears of his mount as his spurs desperately continued to drive into the animal's flesh.

Dust kicked up off the hoofs of the charging horse

as it made its way along the deserted road between the acres of tall swaying grass. Clem had never travelled this way before. When he had ridden to Sioux City he had come from the west; he had never imagined that there were boulders as immense as those towards which he was now racing.

His eyes narrowed as they focused upon the smooth, massive rocks. They grew larger with every beat of his still-pounding heart.

The sound of the riotous town behind him grew fainter the further the veteran lawman rode away from its brught lantern light. Soon the only thing Clem could hear was the constant pounding of his horse's hoofs as they continued to thunder across the frost-hardened ground in search of his friend.

Mile after mile the valiant rider forged on in search of the Valko Kid or the devilish creature who masqueraded as the young man. He had two plans in his head. If he came across Valko he would warn him and if he encountered the Shadow he would try to kill him. Yet there seemed to be no chance of his doing either on the long desolate road.

A road which seemed to be never ending.

Then there was something ahead of him masked by the low-hanging cloud of frosty mist. Something his ancient eyes failed to understand until he was almost upon it.

It was the body of the dead stagecoach's shotgun

guard, lying in the circle of his own gore. The moon-light glistened on the pool of blood.

The rider hauled rein.

His horse stopped immediately just before it reached the lifeless body. It snorted and lowered its head as Clem looked down upon the brutal scene.

The body was twisted and frozen where it had fallen. A stunned expression remained upon its face.

Clem took a deep breath. Then, just as he was about to dismount to check the corpse he heard the plaintive cries of a young woman carried on the night breeze from the distant boulders. They were the same tormented cries that had lured Valko to ride towards the boulders earlier.

Clem swallowed hard, but there was no spittle.

His throat was dry as every sinew in his body tensed in readiness for action. There was no mistaking the sound of a young woman in trouble and Clem knew from experience that if the banker's daughter were in the hands of the Shadow her life would soon end. He had to try and save her, for that was what men of his kind did.

He gritted his teeth and spurred on towards the boulders at breakneck pace. This was a race against time and for the young Polly Wilson time was running out fast.

The horse charged on.

SEVENTEEN

The powerful white stallion had thundered into the rocky labyrinth of trails that spread out from the stagecoach road in all directions like the legs of a spider. Every few yards there seemed to be a narrow trail leading into another unknown maze. The rocks rose up like sleeping giants and towered over the racing stallion as its master searched for tracks of his enemies mount. Another pitiful scream echoed all around the granite rocks.

Valko stopped his horse.

He felt helpless.

'Where is she?' the Kid snarled. His eyes darted all around him. The moonlight did not reach in to most of the trails that surrounded him. Black shadows encompassed half of the countless pathways through the mountain range. The youngster was becoming desperate to find the unknown woman upon whom he had yet to set eyes.

The Kid realized that few women lasted very long when in the company of the evil Shadow. Valko knew he had to find her soon or she would end up the same way as the dead woman he had discovered in the shack earlier.

'Come on, girl,' Valko said as he held the stallion in check and listened hard. 'One more yell and I might be able to figure out where in tarnation you are.'

The sound of the distressed girl's screaming had stopped as suddenly as it had started. Valko looked all around him. The rocks seemed to climb up to the very stars themselves.

'I gotta find her before he. . . .' Valko did not finish his sentence. As though on cue he heard another muffled cry for help ring out from somewhere far above him. The Kid swung the large horse around and vainly tried to work out from which direction the piteous cry had come. It was impossible.

All that was certain was that both the Shadow and his captive were further up the mountain than he had at first thought. Valko gazed around his narrow confines. His eyes burned into the black shadows in search of a trail that would allow him to ascend the gigantic boulders to the place where he might find them both. Once again he had failed.

126

'Damn it all! Another dead end,' Valko cursed angrily. He swiftly turned the white stallion and retraced his tracks to the main road.

Despite the narrowness of the way between the rocks to either side of him, Valko forced the mighty horse to find its best pace through the twisted nightmare in which he was trapped. For Valko knew there was an innocent woman being held prisoner who desperately needed saving before her insane captor became bored and sent her to meet her Maker as he had done to countless others.

Whoever she was the woman needed help quickly, yet the young horseman feared he might never find her. At least, not whilst she was still alive. Valko could see the moonlit sandy road ahead of him. The large white stallion squeezed through the narrow gap in the rocks until it reached it.

The Kid's horse had no sooner stopped on the road than the unexpected sound of an approaching rider to his right caught his attention. The Kid swung on his saddle just as the horseman was upon him. Startled, Valko drew one of his guns at the very same moment as a rifle barrel made violent contact with his head and chest. Valko was knocked backwards and lifted off his saddle. He rolled over the cantle and fell heavily to the ground. He crashed face down into the frosty sand. Then he heard the chilling sound of the horseman's mount circle around him.

Valko shook his head. A thousand war drums had exploded inside his skull. He tried to get to his feet when he heard the horseman dismount beside him. The gun was still in his outstretched hand as a boot was pressed down on his wrist.

Then the dazed Kid felt the cold metal barrel of a six-shooter placed against his temple.

'Move and you're dead man,' the voice growled.

EIGHTEEN

Valko felt a hand grab his collar and bandanna, then jerk his head up off the sand. He was choking but unable to fight back as his attacker's boot pressed down on his wrist. The .45 slowly fell from Valko's clawlike grasp. The pounding inside his skull continued to torment the youngster as the cold steel of his adversary's gun barrel pressed hard into the side of his temple. Valko spat sand from his mouth and then was thrown over on to his back.

He tried to look up into the face of the man who had bested him but it was impossible. The light of the bright moon was directly behind the wide-brimmed Stetson. All the Kid could see was a tall black shape and the cocked gun levelled at his face. A thousand drums kept hampering his thoughts as blood trickled from the corner of his mouth.

Had the Shadow managed to get his hands on him at last?

Was this going to be the end of the trail? Had he been lured into the rocky terrain by the evil Shadow, like a fly to a spider's web?

'Why don't you shoot?' Valko yelled angrily.

There was a silence. The man eased backward and lowered his weapon.

'Valko?' Clem Everett gasped in horror. 'I almost blew your head off.'

'You almost knocked it off first.' Valko rolled on to his knees, then rose unsteadily to his full height. He rubbed his throbbing head in the palms of his hands. 'What did you hit me with?'

'Just my old carbine,' Clem admitted as he drove his gun back into its holster sheepishly. 'Hell. I thought you were the Shadow. I heard me the screaming of a young female and knew that he had kidnapped the banker's daughter. I put two and two together and got my figuring wrong.'

The Kid could not remain angry with his old friend. He patted Clem's shoulder, walked shakily to his horse and grabbed his reins. 'No problem. I heard the same cries as you did. She's up there some-place with him.'

Clem stared to where Valko was pointing. 'How we going to get all the way up there, Kid?'

Valko gave a long deep sigh. 'I've bin asking myself the same thing for the last ten minutes. I've ridden up at least three dead-end draws and gullies and not

130

found anything like a trail. There has to be one.'

'The Shadow found it,' Clem reasoned. 'That means it has to be darn close. Unless he knows the lie of the land a whole lot better than we do, which I surely doubt.'

Valko thought for a moment. The moon was now directly above the stagecoach road, unlike when he had first arrived among the high rocks.

'When I rode in here the road was in shadow. I couldn't see any tracks, but look.' The Kid led his horse to the centre of the road. Even with all the stagecoach tracks across its surface the fresh hoof tracks of their enemy's horse stood out in the glistening frost. 'Do you see them, pard?'

'I sure do.' Clem grabbed his loose reins and led his mount down the middle of the road. Then he paused. He mounted and aimed a gloved finger ahead of them. 'The tracks head down there, towards the bend.'

Even stunned, Valko was able to throw himself up on to the saddle of his high-shouldered stallion in one fluid action. He gathered in his reins and heeled his mount to walk to where Clem awaited. The older man screwed up his eyes and pointed.

'They're coming.'

The Kid looked back at the distant Sioux City. 'Who?'

'A posse and Johnny Sunset.'

'They after me?'

'Yep.'

Valko shrugged. 'Then we better work fast.'

Both horsemen looked at the moonlit sand. The sparkling frost could not conceal the tracks of those who had recently ridden across its surface.

'You ready?' The Kid asked.

'I've bin ready for years, boy.'

The riders urged their mounts forward. They had no sooner started towards the bend than they heard yet another cry echo all around them. Valko leaned back and looked up.

Suddenly he saw the black shape of a man on the very top of the highest of the mighty rocks. A man who had also seen them. Valko was about to point upward when a flash of red lightning burst from the barrel of a six-shooter. A deafening noise filled the riders' ears. Within the blink of an eye a bullet cut into Clem's horse. It made a sickening whinny.

The wounded animal reared up and threw its master. Clem landed hard upon the ground as his mount staggered away and eventually fell into the sand. Blood poured from its wound.

Valko leaned over and grabbed the arm of his friend as another shot was fired down at them. Valko felt its heat as he dragged Clem off the sand and swung him on to his saddle cantle.

'Hang on, Clem,' Valko shouted. More bullets

rained down from the high cliff edge. Valko cracked the tails of his reins. The powerful white stallion obeyed its master and galloped away from where Everett's horse lay dying. Even with an extra passenger on its back the horse lost none of its speed. Without even knowing it the stallion had found the narrow fissure in the wall of otherwise solid rock and had ridden straight into it. Valko hauled rein. Snow stopped as both men leapt to the ground and drew their weapons.

They were in a place where half their surroundings were hidden by shadows and the rest lit up by the eerie moonlight which was creeping over the high boulders to either side. Valko held out an arm and kept his pal well behind him as he studied the strange place.

'I reckon this has to be the route the Shadow used to get up there, Clem,' Valko remarked. He aimed his gun at hoof tracks which led to a trail that took a steep winding course before it disappeared from view behind the hundred-foot high boulder before them.

'Yep,' Clem agreed. 'I don't reckon we'll be able to follow him up there, though.'

Valko looked at his friend. He was about to ask why when another shot cut a fiery trail down from far above them. The bullet shattered on the rocks behind them. The Kid moved back into the blackness and squinted upward. Then he saw the man clad in black waving two guns around. Both guns were smoking.

'You're right, Clem. He's got us pinned down. There ain't no way we can get up that trail without him filling us with lead.' Valko rubbed his still sore jaw thoughtfully. 'Not unless we find another way to get up there.'

'What you mean, Kid?' Clem leaned closer to his young comrade. 'What you got hatching in that head of yours?'

Valko did not answer with words. He smiled and moved back to his horse. Then he removed his cutting rope from the saddle horn and showed it to the veteran lawman. 'Now do you savvy what I'm planning, old-timer?'

Clem raised an eyebrow. 'Reckon we have to catch him before we can hang him, boy.'

Valko shook his head. 'That's right, but it ain't what I've got planned. I reckon the moonlight ain't lit up half that rock he's standing on yet. I got about a half-hour before it does.'

'So?' Clem was still unsure what his pal meant.

'So I can climb up it and he ain't gonna see me, Clem.' Valko smiled. 'I can use this rope to get me from down here to up there. Now do you savvy?'

'That's suicide, Kid,' Clem tokd him. 'The Shadow will pick you off before you get halfway up there and you know it. There has to be a better way.'

134

'If you figure it out, let me know.' Valko handed one of his guns to Everett. 'In the meantime use this and your own hoglegs to give me cover.'

Before the older man could say another word the Kid looped the rope over his shoulder and moved quickly through the darker side of the canyon towards the foot of the gigantic stone rockface. The retired lawman swallowed hard and cocked the hammer of the .45 until it fully locked, then he fired upward. Shots cut through the air in both directions.

Clem kept firing over and over, yet none of his bullets seemed to be able to find their target. There was a pause as both men reloaded their guns. Then Clem heard the sickening laughter. It mocked him as it had mocked countless others over the years.

'You'll have to do a darn sight better than that,' the Shadow bellowed down. 'I don't die easy.'

Clem shook spent casings from the smoking chambers of his guns and reloaded them as quickly as he could. He knew that as long as he kept firing the Shadow might not see or hear the young man who was going to try and climb the wall of rock in order to free the young woman.

Unseen by the villainous killer Valko moved to the very edge of the blackness and shook the rope loop loose. He gazed upward, seeking something to aim at; then he saw it. A jagged rock was poking out from the otherwise smooth boulders about thirty feet from where he stood. That was his target. If he could reach there he knew that he could climb the rest of the rockface until he reached its summit.

Valko had roped steers during his younger days but he had never attempted anything like this. Then he heard the pitiful cries of Polly Wilson once more.

'You can do it this,' Valko told himself. 'You have to do this or that varmint will turn them guns on her.'

The shooting resumed. Deafening echoes filled the gully. The Kid began to rotate the rope as fast as he could until he knew he had the necessary momentum. Then he swung his arm and released the loop. He watched as it flew up and encircled the jagged rock. He tugged on the rope and pulled until the loop tightened.

Then he started his intrepid climb.

NINETEEN

The summit of the rocky heights was redolent with the acrid aroma of gunsmoke. The Shadow stepped back from the cliff edge and stared upon the woman he had tethered to the saddle of his grey. Polly Wilson had fought with her rawhide bonds until her wrists bled but as she watched the fearsome figure move back down the rocky slope towards her with his pair of smoking .45s in his hands she sank to her knees. It was like staring into the face of the Devil. There was no humanity in his hideous features, just evil.

'Reckon you want me to beg,' Polly whimpered. 'Well, I shall never beg a creature like you. Kill me if that's what you want. I no longer care.'

The Shadow paused and dropped one of his guns into its holster. He shook casings from his other smoking gun and searched his gunbelt for fresh bullets.

'Nope. I don't want you to beg me, gal,' he uttered, snapping his gun chamber shut. 'I want you to pleasure me and then die.'

Her eyes burned at him in horror. She wanted to speak but there were no words left in her young mind with which she could express her total confusion.

The Shadow paused beside her and grinned. 'I reckon ya old pa ain't going to cough up the ransom money, gal.'

She squirmed as he touched her bruised face. 'He'll pay you. He loves me. There ain't no call for you to kill me.'

The Shadow leaned over his helpless victim. 'There is.'

'Why would you want to kill me if you get your blood money?' Polly tried to struggle but the rawhide laces were too strong. 'Why?'

'Coz I like killing folks, gal.' The Shadow laughed. Polly tried to shy away from him but the grey horse did not move an inch and held its master's victim in check. She could see the murderous thoughts carved into his brutal features and it frightened her more than anything had ever frightened her before.

Then there was a noise which drew the outlaw's attention and made him straighten up. This noise was not coming from the gully far below the cliff edge but from the road between the range of rocks and Sioux City. The Shadow turned on his heel and ran up the sloping rocks until he reached the highest point of the rocky range. The Shadow screwed up his eyes and glared out through the moonlight down to where he could see a band of at least a half-dozen riders. Their dust hung in the night air.

'I told that damn banker to come here alone,' the Shadow snarled as he reloaded his other gun. 'That's a damn posse.'

Polly remained beside the horse and watched the man clad entirely in black run back towards her. She feared the worst and closed her eyes. The Shadow reached his mount, dragged his Winchester from its scabbard, then returned to where he had spotted his uninvited guests. Polly felt her heart resume its beating inside her chest.

The Shadow pushed the hand guard down and then jerked it up again. A spent casing flew from the Winchester's magazine as the lethal outlaw raised the long-barrelled weapon until its wooden stock rested against his shoulder. He closed one eye and stared through his sights at the horsemen. He squeezed his trigger.

The sound of the rifle being fired resounded around him as the villainous man watched as one of the posse was plucked from his saddle and crashed into the unforgiving ground. He laughed at the confusion among the riders as they suddenly realized that they were under attack.

'Keep on coming,' he growled as he readied the rifle for his next shot. 'I got me plenty of bullets.'

Shot after deadly shot spewed from his rifle barrel as the Shadow expertly cocked and fired in quick succession. By the time his rifle was empty only three horsemen remained in their saddles as they raced toward the cover of the gigantic boulders.

'Keep on coming, boys,' he grunted excitedly. 'There ain't nothing I likes better than a turkey-shoot.'

Johnny Sunset, Chuck Bristow and the terrified Rufe Wilson had reached the first of the massive rocks only a matter of seconds before their attacker had stopped to reload his rifle. They each dismounted and huddled together beneath the protection of one of the boulders. The sheriff felt sweat trailing down his back under his shirt and top coat whilst his unblinking eyes looked back at the dead and wounded men who had been his posse. Wilson dragged his canvas bag from his saddle horn and held it close to his chest and ample belly.

'Why did he start shooting at us, Sheriff?' the terrified Wilson asked the lawman.

Bristow was unable to answer. All he could do was stare at the bodies scattered across the stagecoach road.

Wilson shook Bristow's arm. 'Answer me. Why did Valko open up on us like that?'

Sunset cautiously eased away from the rocks and tried to see the man who had nearly wiped them all out. 'Stop gabbing.'

The banker glared at the bounty hunter. 'I beg your pardon? Do you know who I am?'

Sunset eyed Wilson up and down. 'Yep. You're the *hombre* that wet his pants. Now shut the hell up and let me do what I come here to do.'

Wilson inhaled deeply. 'And what did you come here to do?'

Johnny Sunset grabbed hold of the saddle horn and swung up on to the back of the horse. The bounty hunter gathered his reins up, then replied:

'I come here to kill the Valko Kid.'

Both men watched as Johnny Sunset slapped leather and thundered away. Bristow rubbed his sweating jowls, then turned to the wide-eyed banker who still nursed the bag swollen with money.

'Reckon he might just do it, Rufe.'

TWENTY

The Shadow ran back down to his horse and the woman slumped beside it. He opened the nearer satchel of his saddle-bags and pulled out a full box of rifle bullets. He paused and stared down at his helpless victim. It was like a fox studying a chicken trapped in its henhouse. He laughed at her, and her tear-stained eyes gazed up at him. For one so young Polly had lost all hope of surviving this night. She could not imagine anything except death awaiting her before sunrise.

'Why are you going to kill me?'

The Shadow roared at her with insane amusement. 'I told you, gal. I'm going to kill you coz I can. It ain't nothing personal, you understand.'

For the first time since encountering the outlaw, rage replaced fear inside the young woman's soul. She forced herself up off the sand, then furiously spat at him. It was her only weapon.

With spittle clinging to his face the outraged Shadow suddenly felt his anger erupt. He gritted his teeth and lashed out at her furiously. The box of rifle bullets caught the side of her face and knocked her out. Only the rawhide restraints which kept her hands tethered to his saddle stopped her from falling to the ground. She was suspended like a stringed puppet.

The Shadow grunted, then turned and ran back up the cliff edge where he started to reload his Winchester once more. As her saliva dripped from his hideous features he resumed his firing at the distant law officers.

It took every scrap of Valko's dwindling strength to haul himself up on to the jutting ledge on the rock-face. As more shots rang out from the Shadow's rifle and the Kid's vengeful impersonator continued to fire down at what remained of the posse Valko cautiously rose to his feet and steadied himself. One false move and he knew he would fall. A fall could only end in one of two ways. One was death: the other was even worse. It was to be broken and crippled.

Valko looked up briefly. He was within twenty feet of reaching the top of the huge boulder and he could hear the voice of his adversary as he ranted and mocked the distant posse. The Kid knew that he had to use his rope again if he were to scale the almost smooth rock and get his hands on the Shadow. With the echoing of the rifle shots ringing in the Kid's ears he pulled the slack of his cutting rope up until he could balance on the narrow ledge.

Valko looped the rope around his hand and elbow until he had its entire coiled length in his control. He then cautiously rested his sweat-soaked spine against the rocks and tried to get his breath back as he concentrated on the distance between himself and his goal.

He made a wide loop again and tried to find a target to aim at. There was not a lot of choice. Only one cracked part of the cliff edge looked as though it might be possible to lasso. The trouble was that his target was bathed in moonlight, which might betray him before he was able to clamber up on to the flat surface of the cliff top and confront the deadly Shadow. It was a chance the Kid was willing to take. It had to end this night, Valko thought. One way or another, it had to end here.

Valko started to swing the rope loop around and around until it started to buzz like a nest of angry hornets. Then he released it and watched as the loop left the darkness and encircled the crack in the rocks above him. He jerked the rope until it was taut, then tied the other end around his chest. He made a firm knot and took hold of the rope in his gloved hands.

Once again he started to ascend the huge boulder. Once again every sinew in his body screamed out in agony. He glanced down and caught a glimpse of his old pal in the shadows beside his trusty horse. Then returned his attention to the job in hand and continued climbing.

Far below, Clem Everett took hold of the reins of the white stallion and was about to mount when he heard the sound of pounding hoofs out on the stage-coach road. He looked through the natural crack in the rockface and saw the bounty hunter thundering past the well-hidden entrance.

'Sunset,' Clem whispered to himself. 'It won't take that *hombre* long to find this place.'

He swung round on his boot heels and knew that whilst the Shadow was distracted by the distant posse this would perhaps be his only opportunity to take the trail to the mountain summit and confront him. Yet Clem realized that he dare not take the white stallion. If Johnny Sunset clapped eyes upon it he would instantly recognize it.

Clem led the mighty horse deeper into the black shadows and tied its reins to a jagged boulder. He then raced as best he could to the steep trail and started to make his way up to where the rifle shots still rang out far above him. Clem knew that it was a perilous thing for anyone to attempt and if the

Shadow realized what was happening he would again turn his guns upon him, yet like his young friend the retired marshal was ready to take the risk.

He had noticed that there had not been any pitiful cries for quite some time from the Shadow's victim. He wondered why.

There was only one way to find out. Clem Everett kept moving up the steep incline with guns drawn.

TWENTY-ONE

Gripping the rope tightly in his gloved hands Valko threw his leg over the rocky rim of the great boulder and scrambled on to its flat surface. He was exhausted but knew that there was no time to dwell on his own troubles; now he had to settle a score which was long overdue. The Kid rested on one knee and stared at the back of his adversary through the eerie blue light of the bright moon. He was within forty feet of the insane impostor. The Shadow continued firing his rifle at men who were already dead on the edge of the mountain range. Valko had only one of his matched Colt .45s with him but knew that if his aim was true six bullets were more than enough.

As the Kid rose to his full height he noticed the forlorn figure of the young woman beside the grey horse at the foot of the steep incline of rock. She was motionless and Valko feared that his desperate climb had been in vain. Had he arrived too late to save her? The question burned inside him like a branding-iron.

Valko's thumb flicked the leather safety loop from the holstered gun hammer as he valiantly began to walk across the smooth rock toward the Shadow. The end of his cutting rope was still secured around his heaving chest under his armpits, but he knew there was no time to release it. He removed his right glove, tucked it into his belt and flexed his fingers above the holstered weapon.

Valko was now within twenty feet of the Shadow's back as the remorseless murderer continued to fire his rifle at the men he had pinned down on the stage-coach road.

It was only when the Shadow's index finger tugged on the Winchester's trigger and the rifle failed to spew out another lethal bullet that Valko paused and spoke.

'Why don't you turn and draw on me?' the Kid said in a low, fearless drawl. 'Scared of folks that can shoot back?'

The Shadow recognized the voice. The voice of the youngster he had managed to brand with all of his own crimes for so long. It had been a long time since they had encountered one another but the memories, like the scars, remained with each of them.

'Valko?' The Shadow uttered the name as he turned slowly round to face the Kid. A cruel smile covered his features. 'I just knew it had to happen one day. One day you'd get lucky and catch up with me.'

Valko took a deep breath. His fingers continued to move above his gun grip. 'Now it ends. It ends here.'

'It'll never end, boy.' The Shadow tossed the rifle aside and raised both his hands until they were hovering over his own pair of Colts. 'I'd have to die for it to end and the only one who'll die today is you.'

'I'm going to kill you,' Valko vowed. 'I should have done it a long time back when I had you in my sights.'

The Shadow sneered. 'You ain't got the guts, Valko. You couldn't kill me then and you ain't going to do it now. You just ain't got what it takes to be a real man.'

The Valko Kid felt sweat run from his black hat band and trail down his face. He knew that the Shadow was right. In all his days he had never killed anyone unless they had been trying to kill him. To shoot someone, even someone as bad as the creature before him, was entirely alien to him.

'Draw,' Valko said.

The Shadow laughed out loud. 'Why don't *you* draw, Kid? Why? I reckon it's coz I'm right and you just can't do it.'

Valko stared hard at the deadly man. A man who, he knew, took pleasure from torturing him. 'I said draw and I meant it.'

'You can't do it, boy.' The Shadow began to pace slowly towards the Kid. His mocking laughter grew louder with each step. The distance between them shrank until the two men were within an arm's length of one another. 'Still can't kill any critter who ain't already shooting at you. Can you?'

Valko knew his brutal impostor was correct. He could never draw and fire on someone who had not already started to shoot at him first.

'Shoot, Valko. Shoot or I'll beat you to within an inch of your life,' the Shadow warned. 'I'll whip you like a mangy dog and make you beg for me to stop.'

Suddenly Valko clenched his fists. 'You want to fight? I'll oblige you.'

The evil outlaw's head was knocked backwards as Valko's right fist caught the jaw of the man in front of him. The Shadow staggered, then grunted. He ducked the next two punches, then swung an upper-cut which sent the younger man tumbling head over heels.

The Shadow raced after his opponent and kicked out with the toe of his pointed left boot. The Kid was lifted off the rocky surface of the rocks. He cart-wheeled back another half-dozen feet before coming to a rest on his knees. Blood dripped from his mouth as the Kid squinted through the moonlight at the man who was charging towards him like a raging bull.

Somehow, just as the older man reached him, Valko leapt back on to his feet and blocked the next vicious punch. He leaned to his side and struck the Shadow in the ribs. He saw the horror in the face of his foe as yet another frenzied attack slammed into him. Fists and boots driven by a strength that only the insane possess smashed into the Kid. He was dazed as one punch after another found its target.

Blow after blow connected with Valko's chin. He staggered backwards as the frenetic onslaught continued. The Shadow was like a champion prizefighter dishing out a boxing lesson to a young upstart. The Kid tried to defend himself but it was useless. He was soaking up every punch and kick the Shadow was dishing out.

Valko fell. He was close to the cliff edge, where his rope was firmly secured. He shook his head and blinked hard. All he could see was the man in black striding towards him.

The man had drawn one of his guns and was aiming it at his latest victim.

'You going to kill me?' Valko spat blood on to the rocks at his knees as he shakily staggered to his feet. 'I thought you wanted to torture me a while longer? You can't torture a dead man.'

The Shadow stopped and thrust the gun back into its holster. 'You're dead right, boy. There ain't no fun in wrecking the life of a corpse. As long as you're alive I can keep on doing my worst knowing nobody will ever blame me.'

Valko's right eye was swollen and closing fast. His vision was becoming blurred but he did not intend to quit now. He pointed at Polly Wilson.

'Is she dead?'

'Not yet.'

A sense of relief swept through the battered and bruised Kid. He had not arrived too late, as he had thought. There was still a chance for her, yet he knew it was a mighty slim one.

'You got a name?' The Kid asked as he swayed. 'Even a damn stinking critter like you must have a name.'

'Sure thing.' The Shadow smiled and poked a finger into the chest of his opponent. The Kid felt himself being forced back until his boot heels were on the very rim of the cliff.

'What is it? What's your damn name?' Valko repeated. 'After everything you've done to me I've got the right to know who you are.'

The Shadow raised a boot and kicked out. He caught the Kid in the belly. The ferocity of the kick pushed the younger man off the top of the boulder. Suddenly Valko was falling. His arms clawed at the air but to no avail.

The Shadow looked down over the edge of the cliff and watched in amusement as the rope tightened and the Kid came to a painful halt in mid-air. 'What's my name? Hell, I'm the Valko Kid.'

Clem Everett had managed to reach halfway up the steep incline when he heard the horse charging up behind him. Clem paused and stared at the bounty hunter as Sunset stopped his mount beside him.

'You going to let me ride with you, Sunset?' Clem held out a hand to the bounty hunter but Johnny Sunset ignored it and rose in his stirrups.

'And let you warn that stinking friend of yours, Everett?' Sunset sneered. 'I don't think so.'

The veteran lawman watched as the rider lashed his horse with the tails of his reins and thundered away. Clem shook his head and continued staggering up the steep trail in pursuit. Time was running out for every living soul on the mountain and Clem Everett knew it.

The rope cut deeply into the flesh under Valko's arms as the Kid suddenly realized he was dangling helplessly above a deadly drop. He was spinning around at the end of the long cutting rope like a child's toy. His hands grabbed hold of the rope and gripped its rough fibres as his long legs stretched and

somehow managed to find the wall of rock. Valko
stopped spinning and steadied himself. He gazed up
at the figure in black who was still laughing down at
him.

Then something drew the attention of the outlaw
away from his helpless victim. Valko watched as the
Shadow turned from the edge of the cliff and walked
out of view. The Kid mustered every ounce of what
strength he had remaining in his brutalized body
and started to haul himself up again towards the
cracked rock that his rope was looped around.

The Shadow's attention had returned to his young
prisoner as she stirred and began to cough. No
sooner had he started to walk towards her than he
heard another noise: a more disturbing noise. It was
the unmistakable sound of hoofs as they echoed off
the rocks that flanked the trail up to the high
summit. The deadly outlaw rested his wrists on the
grips of his holstered guns and started to move faster
towards his prisoner and his horse. His spurs rang
out as his pace quickened. He was within spitting distance of the grey when he saw the horseman
thunder out of the blackness into the bright moonlight. The Shadow stopped and swung around to
face the unknown intruder. His hands went for his
guns.

Johnny Sunset leaned back and drew his reins up to

his chest as his eyes adjusted to the bright moonlight. Two shots cut through the night air. The sound of the young woman screaming in terror filled the bounty hunter's ears at the very moment his left shoulder was punched back by a bullet.

The Shadow watched the bounty hunter fall into the dust and raced towards him. He cocked both hammers and fired his guns again. The ground kicked up as the bullets narrowly missed their target. Defying his own pain Sunset rolled across the ground under the belly of his mount. The horse reared up, then its hoofs came crashing down a few inches from the bounty hunter's bleeding shoulder.

The Shadow leaned down to his right and cocked his smoking guns once more. Only gunsmoke separated the two men as Sunset hastily dragged the hefty modified scattergun from its reinforced holster.

Two more deafening shots sped on their way from the barrels of the deadly outlaw as he advanced on the man lying on the sand. The prostrate bounty hunter felt the heat from the bullets as they buried themselves into the ground close to his already blood-soaked shoulder.

Sunset's skittish mount dropped its head and charged the Shadow. The outlaw leapt out of its path just as Johnny Sunset managed to struggle up on to his knees.

The sight of the mighty gun confused the outlaw for a split second. That was all the time Sunset needed to squeeze both of the weapon's triggers.

The scorching fury of the scattergun's blast caught the Shadow full in his face. The outlaw was dead before his body crashed into the ground beside the banker's terrified daughter. There was little left of what had once been his face but the wounded Johnny Sunset was convinced that he had achieved his goal. He had killed the Valko Kid.

Sunset staggered to what remained of the Shadow, then leaned over and freed Polly Wilson from her bonds. She got to her feet and shied away from the sight before them.

'You know his name?' Sunset asked through his pain.

Polly Wilson nodded and began to sob. 'Valko. He said his name was Valko.'

'Thanks, ma'am.' Sunset smiled as he saw Clem Everett emerge from the darkness. 'That's all I wanted to know.'

Everett did not stop until he was standing over the body clad in black. For a moment he thought that it was his pal, then he noticed the spurs on the boots. Clem knew his pal never wore spurs.

Sunset looked into Clem's face. 'I got him, Everett. I killed the Valko Kid.'

The veteran lawman inhaled deeply and glanced

around the barren area. His attention returned to the dealy bounty hunter. He nodded.

'Reckon you did, Sunset.'

FINALE

The morning sun spread its light and warmth across the top of the high rocky vista and the scene of bloody retribution. Clem Everett sat silently on the slope with his back to the cliff edge and watched as the triumphant bounty hunter secured the blood-soaked body of the Shadow across the grey horse's saddle. He lashed the boots and hands of the dead man to the stirrups on either side of the horse, then drew his own hired animal close to him and the still shocked young woman. Johnny Sunset stepped into the stirrup of his mount and hoisted himself up in to the saddle. He offered a stirrup to young Polly; she accepted it and quickly climbed up behind the bounty hunter.

Sunset was wounded but you would never have known it were it not for the gore that covered the sleeve of his topcoat. He refused to allow anyone ever to see even a hint of weakness.

'How do you figure on getting back to Sioux City, old-timer?' Sunset asked the silent lawman. 'You could ride the grey if you don't mind sharing with your dear dead friend.'

Clem stood. There was no emotion in his wrinkled features.

'Nope. I ain't going back there.'

Sunset was curious. 'But you ain't got a mount. How'd you figure on getting anywhere on foot?'

'That's my problem.' Clem smiled. 'Don't go fretting about me, Sunset. You go and collect your damn blood money.'

Sunset felt the woman's arms wrap thenselves around his waist and hold on tightly. He spurred and rode away from the old lawman. Within seconds the bounty hunter had disappeared down the steep trail, leading the grey and its grisly cargo.

Only when he was satisfied that Sunset had truly gone did Clem turn and rush to the cliff edge. He looked down and saw Valko climbing up the last few feet of the perilous rockface. He reached out a helping hand and dragged his friend up over the side of the rocky rim. He watched as the sorely battered figure fell on his back in total exhaustion.

'It sure took you a while to come help me, Clem,' Valko complained. 'I've bin hanging there trying to reach here for over an hour. What kept you?'

Clem patted the Kid's shoulder and started to untie the rope which had torn through Valko's shirt to expose the bleeding flesh. 'Johnny Sunset was here. I had to wait for him to go.'

Valko raised his head. 'Where's the Shadow?'

'Dead,' Clem answered. 'Sunset blew his head apart with a real fancy gun. You wanna know the funny thing?'

'What, Clem?'

'He reckons he's killed the Valko Kid.' Clem raised his eyebrows. 'He's even taken the body back to Sioux City to claim the reward money.'

Valko sat upright. He could no longer feel any of the pain that had tortured him for so many hours. He grinned.

'That is funny, Clem,' The Kid agreed wryly. 'The Shadow told me he was the Valko Kid. At least someone believed the varmint.'

'Dead right, Kid.' Clem chuckled. 'Dead right.'